The Lord is a refuge for the oppressed,
a stronghold in times of trouble.
—*Psalms* 9:9

This book is dedicated to my husband. He's my Prince Charming, best friend and cheerleader all rolled into one.

ONE

Julianne Grace bristled, pausing mid-step as she journeyed down the lonely road. She froze as her eyes scanned the area in front of her. Woods and swampland surrounded her, but nothing else.

There was the sound again. A stick cracking. Her pulse pounded in her ears as she turned her head. Fear pricked her skin. What had caused the noise?

All she saw was a desolate stretch of highway and looming oak trees enveloped by dark, murky water.

She ran a shaky hand through her mane of hair. She'd heard something. She knew she had. Was someone watching her from the woods?

Could it be Darrell Lewis?

The thought made her blood go cold—cold enough to rival the frigid wind that swept across the deceitfully sunny landscape. She should have worn a coat, but she'd left her apartment too quickly. She hadn't had time to think—just to drive. Now the scar across her collarbone pulled tight in the twenty-degree briskness.

The injury was a daily reminder of how ugly love could turn. A daily reminder of how relationships weren't worth it. Not then. Not now. Not ever.

She took a few more tentative steps. The feeling of unseen eyes caused her pace to quicken until she burst into a jog and then an all-out run. Though she saw nothing and no one, she couldn't shake the feeling that she was being chased.

Finally, a gate appeared in the distance. Could it be the entrance to Iron, Incorporated? Was help in sight?

She could make it that far. She'd ask to see Bradley Stone and then tell him the truth about why she'd come. She'd ask the burning questions that consumed her and hopefully get some answers.

She had to get what she'd come for. She had no other options, not if she wanted to live to see tomorrow.

Her legs felt like jelly when she reached the guardhouse. Her quick breaths came out in icy clouds, and she shivered again. What a mess. Everything was a mess.

A fresh-faced man in uniform stared at her. She could tell by the way his eyes wavered from side to side for just a split second that her presence baffled him. Certainly people didn't tread up to the

"I saw someone outside. Did you see anything? Hear anything?" Bradley asked.

Julianne shook her head, fear spreading through her. "Nothing. Just you."

He offered a crisp nod. "Stay put. And call the police if I don't return within the hour."

"If you don't...?" She shut her mouth and nodded, not wanting to think about the implications of what he was saying. "Okay."

She closed the door and turned the locks, checking each latch twice. Three times, for that matter. Then she backed away from the door. She kept backing up until she hit a wall. She stood there, frozen to the spot, her eyes darting around from one window to the next. She expected to see shadows, to hear yells and footfalls, to flinch from the sound of gunshot.

Instead, she heard nothing.

Was her ex-fiancé out there? Had he found her? What about Bradley? Was he hurt?

Books by Christy Barritt

Love Inspired Suspense

Keeping Guard
The Last Target
Race Against Time
Ricochet
*Key Witness
*Lifeline

*The Security Experts

CHRISTY BARRITT

loves stories and has been writing them for as long as she can remember. She gets her best ideas when she's supposed to be paying attention to something else—like in a workshop or while driving down the road.

The second book in her Squeaky Clean Mystery series, *Suspicious Minds,* won the inspirational category of the 2009 Daphne du Maurier Award for Excellence in Suspense and Mystery. She's also the coauthor of *Changed: True Stories of Finding God in Christian Music.*

When she's not working on books, Christy writes articles for various publications. She's also a weekly feature writer for the *Virginian-Pilot* newspaper, the worship leader at her church and a frequent speaker at various writers' groups, women's luncheons and church events.

She's married to Scott, a teacher and funny man extraordinaire. They have two sons, two dogs and a houseplant named Martha.

To learn more about her, visit her website, www.christybarritt.com.

LIFELINE

CHRISTY BARRITT

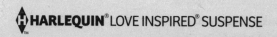

Recycling programs
for this product may
not exist in your area.

™ LOVE INSPIRED BOOKS

ISBN-13: 978-0-373-67567-8

LIFELINE

www.LoveInspiredBooks.com

Printed in U.S.A.

gate every day, not when you considered there were miles of empty road before reaching the compound.

"Can I help you?" The guard was short, blond and had a gun at his waist. His gaze roamed behind her, as if her appearance were some kind of guerrilla-war tactic.

"I need to see Bradley Stone." The words were labored, partially from her jog and partially from fear. "It's important. Very important."

The man blinked, and his face remained devoid of expression. "Bradley Stone? Your name?"

"Julianne Grace." Her breathing still hadn't normalized. Her shivers reached her vocal cords, causing her voice to crack.

"Do you have an appointment?"

She shook her head, the reality that she may not be able to see him sinking in. But she couldn't retreat now. "No, I don't. But I need to talk to him. Please. I've come four hours to get here, all the way from D.C."

His lips pulled into a tight line. "One moment."

He stepped into the small brick booth and picked up a phone. Julianne rubbed her palms on her jeans. Despite the chill, she'd still managed to break a sweat.

She turned, glanced behind her. Nothing. What did she think she would see? Darrell hiding behind a tree? The thought was ridiculous.

But she'd heard a branch break. Had an animal made the sound? Or was it the man bent on tormenting her?

She rubbed her clammy hands against her jeans. She couldn't dislodge the thoughts from her mind. Thoughts of pain and death at the hands of a man who liked to see others suffer. Was there any other reason Darrell had thrown acid on her, hoping to hit her face and disfigure her so that no other man would want her?

The guard approached her, that inscrutable expression still across his face. "I'm sorry, but Mr. Stone can't speak with you now. He told me to give you the number of his secretary so that you could schedule an appointment."

Tears sprung to her eyes. She tried to hold them off, but it did no good. Her gaze met the guard's. The last thing she wanted was to manipulate the situation, but she had to make her desperation clear. "My life depends on it."

"I'm sorry, ma'am." The man handed her a card. A moment of sympathy glimmered in his eyes. "Here's the number for his secretary."

She took the paper from him and crumbled it. She used her sleeve to wipe away her tears as she turned on her heel. What would she do now? Hike back to a gasless car located miles from nothing?

She had to see Bradley Stone. But how?

What were her options? She could scale the fence surrounding the headquarters and make a run for it. Then she remembered the barbed wire atop the iron prongs. Probably not the best idea....

Could she somehow make it past the guard? If she could slip by him and make it to the building in the background maybe Bradley would have no choice but to speak with her.

Right now, she had nothing to lose. Two people were already dead. She'd be next if she didn't get some answers. Either way she looked at it, her life was on the line.

Julianne swallowed so hard that it hurt. She was a peace-loving woman who hated making scenes or adding drama to life. But desperate times called for desperate measures, as the saying went.

She paused and turned toward the guard. "Excuse me, sir. Do you think I could use your phone? Please? I need to call a tow truck. My car ran out of gas and the nearest gas station has to be miles from here."

The guard shifted, his hesitation evident. Her cell phone was tucked into her back pocket, out of sight. She'd never said she didn't have a phone. Still, guilt pressed in on her.

Finally, the young guard nodded and motioned for her to go into the booth. "Just one call."

She nodded, relief washing through her, but quickly replaced as anxiety crowded it out. Did she really think this would work? Regardless, she had to give it a shot.

Lord, protect me, even if I'm being foolish.

She stepped into the booth and picked up the receiver.

Before the guard realized what was happening, she darted through the opposite door and onto the grounds of the Eyes headquarters.

She ran as if her life depended on it.

Because her life did depend on it.

Bradley Stone hung up the phone and leaned back in his desk chair. Julianne Grace. It had been a long time since he'd heard that name. Honestly, he thought he'd never hear it again. Why should he? His military career had ended, Darrell Lewis had died...and his life had begun the proverbial next chapter.

He stood and plucked open two slats from the window blinds. From his office, he could see the front gate.

Why had he sent the woman away? He should feel obligated to speak with her. After all, her fiancé had died on his watch. Most people in his position would bend over backward in this situation.

But Darrell Lewis had had an edge to him, and his death still haunted him to this day. Bradley had tried desperately to put that part of his life behind him. Probably because it included mourning the death of his own fiancée who'd been murdered not even a year after Darrell died.

He knew how it felt to lose someone you loved. He knew what it was like for someone to be snatched away from life before their time.

He didn't want to see Julianne and be reminded again.

He narrowed his eyes as she took a step away from the guard station. Where was her car? Had the woman walked here? Why had she wanted to see him of all people?

He watched as she turned and approached the guardhouse again. She talked to the guard a moment and he pointed toward the gate. Then Julianne walked into the station. What was she doing?

The next instant, she darted across the lawn toward the main building. Bradley straightened as he watched her run as if the ground itself was on fire. The woman was going to get herself killed.

He sprinted from his office. After taking the stairs by two, he rounded the corner and opened the door at the front entrance. He stepped outside just in time to see Julianne fall to the ground. Had she been shot? Terror raced through him.

Eric, the guard, stood with his gun drawn by the gate.

Bradley cupped his hands around his mouth. "Hold your fire!"

Had the woman gone mad? He rushed toward her and knelt on the lawn at her side. She pushed herself up on her elbows, blood trickling from her forehead. She must have hit it on the edge of the pavement.

Her panic-stricken eyes met his. "I need your help."

"You're going to need a lawyer's help also, pulling a stunt like that." He gently gripped her arms as he helped her back to her feet.

"Th-thank you," she stuttered. She brushed a hair behind her ear, as if trying to compose herself. It didn't work. The woman was a wild mess, her limbs like jelly. Her legs gave out, and she started sinking to the ground again when he caught her. Tantalizing eyes met his. "Do you remember me?"

He straightened. "Of course I do. Darrell Lewis's fiancée. What were you thinking charging through the front gate like that?"

Her breath came in deep gasps and her hands trembled. Her long brown hair, streaked with gold, fell into her perfectly proportioned face. But her stunning beauty took a backseat to the fear and desperation that seemed to emanate from her. "Please. I only need a few minutes."

Would she accuse him of her fiancé's death? Maybe. Could he deny he was at fault? No. The responsibility fell on his shoulders alone.

Would she make further inquiries about his death? Possibly. She'd never asked many questions in the first place except, "Are you sure he's dead?"

An odd question, really. Most want to know how

their loved one died, or if they'd experienced any pain or what their last moments had been like.

But she'd asked, "Are you sure?"

He shook the thoughts from his head and glanced at Julianne again. Something about the woman and her wide, luminous eyes tugged at his heart—and he felt himself softening toward her.

He glanced at his watch. His meeting started in five minutes.

Five minutes.

He could give the woman that much.

Most likely, he'd regret it if he didn't. His mind would be flooded with questions about why she had come. The easiest solution to that was to simply talk to her, find out what she wanted, and send her on her way.

"Let's get you out of the cold." He led her inside the large, lodgelike building. Flames blazed from the massive fireplace that stretched upward two stories, giving the lobby a warm, cozy feel. His fingers grazed her hands and he felt the frigidness of her skin. She trembled uncontrollably. Where was her coat?

He kept a hand on her elbow until she reached a leather chair situated by the roaring fireplace. "Why don't you have a seat? Can I get you some coffee? Anything?"

She lowered herself into the seat, her hands quivering against her legs. "Yes, please. If you don't mind. I—I wasn't prepared to be here. This wasn't exactly on my schedule for today."

Just what had brought her here, then? What had caused her to risk her life to speak with him? "Sit tight. Warm up. I'll be right back with that coffee and some first aid for that cut."

He took a step away when Julianne's soft voice cut through the air.

"Actually, I just need to ask you one question. It can't wait."

Bradley pivoted and saw her sitting on the edge of her seat, looking as if she might break at any moment. "One question? Okay, shoot."

She swallowed, stark fear straining her features. "Are you sure Darrell Lewis died during that training exercise?"

Julianne watched Bradley's expression—stone cold, as usual. She'd always thought the name was appropriate for someone who kept such a tight reign on his emotions. He was like an exquisitely carved statue from Roman times. All hard lines and stiff features and breathtaking good looks.

No hint of softness to him.

Bradley Stone was the only person she could think of who might have some answers. He was Darrell's former commanding officer and SEAL platoon OIC—officer-in-charge. He was the one who'd come to her with the news of Darrell's death.

She remembered when he'd shown up at her doorstep, a sympathetic look in his eyes as he held his hat in hand. On either side of him were a chaplain and the CACO—the Casualty Assistance Calls Officer. As soon as she'd seen Bradley, she'd known what was coming. She'd known also that he didn't have to be there, that he could have easily sent the other two men to notify her of what had happened.

She'd met the man twice before that day. He was the strong, silent type with striking blue eyes that showed a perceptive intelligence. Julianne would bet that he didn't miss much. He had a no-nonsense haircut, a tall, broad build that tapered to narrow hips, and a chiseled, smooth face.

His voice had been kind when he'd told her the news about Darrell. As she'd listened, shock had washed over her, shock followed by relief. Tears had rushed to her eyes, and she'd hoped they'd looked like tears of sorrow. But the moisture along her eyelids was because she realized she didn't have to live in fear anymore.

Yet here she was, two years later, living in absolute fear again.

Snapping back to the present, she tried unsuccessfully to read Bradley's expression. All she could see were his eyes, ever perceptive, soaking her in. Finally, after a moment of contemplation, he stepped forward and lowered himself into the chair across from her, the fireplace softening his features.

"Am I sure that your fiancé is dead?" he repeated, his voice even. The man thought she was losing her mind. That was all there was to it. She might think the same thing if she didn't know what she did, if she hadn't seen the things she'd seen.

She nodded, her throat scratchy, and the tremors that had begun in her hands migrating until her entire body shook. "That's right."

He leaned forward, his elbows on his knees, and sucked in a deep breath. He was trying to be diplomatic, trying to measure his response. All professional, she thought with a silent, bitter laugh. Concealing how he really felt in an effort to placate her.

Another round of tears washed through her eyes. She had to get a grip. She was usually so careful to control her emotions, to not appear weak in front of others. They'd only take advantage of you if you did.

But how could she get a grip right now? She couldn't, not until she had some answers. Ignoring her achy head and growling stomach, she directed a steady gaze toward Bradley to let him know she was serious.

His jaw flexed, and he shifted his weight before answering. "I saw your fiancé during explosives training. I saw him go up in flames. I saw his body, half of his bones broken and skin burned to a crisp."

That was the story she'd heard also. But was there room for error there? Was there any possibility of a cover-up? "There was unaccounted-for time. From the moment you realized there was an emergency until the moment you reached him, the bodies could have been switched."

He blinked as if trying to conceal his real thoughts from her. "There was an autopsy."

"But how thorough was it? His fingerprints were nonexistent. Half of his teeth were broken from the impact, so how could you compare dental records even?" She nervously rubbed her loafers across the plush rug at her feet.

Bradley's gaze remained unwavering. "We were certain that the man we found was Darrell. We hated it as much as you did. He was one of our men, and there's nothing worse than losing one of your own. As hard as that news might be to accept, as much as you might want to hold on to the hope that he's alive, it's just not possible."

Julianne shook her head. "No, you're wrong. I don't want him to be alive. But I'm afraid he is."

"Why would you think that?"

"Because he killed two people. And I'm afraid he might want to kill me, too."

TWO

"So let me get his straight. Your fiancé is not only alive, but he's trying to kill you?"

Bradley had been trying to be levelheaded, fair-minded, and to offer at least a touch of compassion to the skittish woman sitting in front of him. But she wanted to confirm the death of her fiancé for fear he might be alive and dangerous? Normal, sane people didn't think like that. Still, he knew what grief could do to a person.

Grief had led him to an isolated existence. He poured every minute of his time now into his work and tried to avoid most social activities. Seeing other couples together reminded him too much of what he'd lost. His faith in God had been the only thing to get him through some dark days.

He stared at Julianne another moment. He should have stuck to his meeting. Turned her away. But instead he'd forgotten his sensibilities and agreed to talk with her. Now what did he say? How could he send her on her way and, at the same time, suggest she get some professional help?

She raised her chin, a measure of defiance kicking in. "I'm not crazy."

He didn't know about that. The woman might be beautiful, but looks could belie lots of other problems. She appeared sweet and innocent on the outside, but what was going on in the inside? Crazy mental problems? Some kind of disorder? Blood trickled from her forehead. Had her fall affected her reasoning?

A group of law-enforcement trainees chattered as they passed by on their way to the cafeteria. The week was packed here at Eyes between the various trainings occurring on campus and several high-level meetings concerning his project.

He had to say something. He pulled his lips into a line before exhaling slowly. "I can assure you, Ms. Grace, that not only is Darrell dead, but he's not capable of killing anyone in his present state—not even you."

She shook her head, another round of tears cascading down her cheeks. He grabbed a box of tissues and nudged them her way, resisting his urge to glance at his watch. He knew he was late for his meeting, and he didn't see how he was ever going to tie up this conversation and get on with his job. Dealing with emotional women had never been his strength, nor was it even remotely in his comfort zone.

"I'm not crazy."

Wasn't that the first thing every insane person said? How could he possibly help this woman? "I didn't say you were."

"No, but you're thinking it." Her eyes lit with fire. "I have to admit, I can't even blame you. I know I sound crazy. But you haven't seen or experienced the things that I have."

"Do you want to tell me about any of those things?" Now why did he have to ask that? Why was he allowing this woman to pull at his heartstrings?

She leaned back, despair twisting her features. She sat silent in thought for a moment, as if running through her options. Finally, she ran a hand over her face. "Can I have that coffee first?"

A chance to get away and clear his head sounded perfect. Besides, he had to call about rescheduling his meeting, as well as file an incident report since Julianne had breached their headquarters. All an enemy had to do was send a damsel in distress, he realized. What red-blooded male wouldn't fall for that? "Absolutely. Do you take anything in it?"

"No. Black is fine."

He walked briskly to the cafeteria area off the lobby. He bypassed the trainees in line and grabbed two mugs, filling them with piping-hot coffee. Not as good as the strong brews he'd had in the military, but it sufficed.

What would the woman say now? Should he even attempt to set her straight? Or should he let her believe her lies and let someone else pop her deluded bubble?

He didn't know. In the end, he'd just have to trust his gut after he heard what she had to say. He paused by the cafeteria's entrance, one eye on Julianne as he put a call in to his boss to let him know what was going on. Then he carried the ceramic mugs back into the lobby where he saw Julianne sitting with her knees pulled up to her chest. Her eyes had a far-away look about them, but the way she flinched as he approached made it clear she was on edge.

Bradley set her coffee on the table between them. He watched as she raised the mug to her lips, her hands shaking so badly he doubted she'd be able to actually take a sip. He said nothing, though.

He lowered himself back into the same chair. After Julianne had put the cup back on the table, he leaned toward her, trying his best to appear diplomatic and at ease. "Why don't you tell me what you're thinking?"

Her gaze seemed to grow more hollow by the minute. Was the woman on drugs? Or was she truly just scared senseless? She licked her lips before starting.

"Two weeks ago, a man I know was killed in an auto accident. The circumstances surrounding his death were suspicious. There was no apparent reason for him to run off the road and hit a tree. No bad weather, no alcohol in his system, no cell phone in his hand. Nothing. By itself, that doesn't sound strange. I know that." She shivered and rubbed her arms. "But this morning, my boss didn't show up for work. He's never missed a day in the year that I've known him. When he didn't call or answer his phone, I got worried and decided to stop by his apartment."

"Go on." He took a sip of his coffee, needing an extra dose of caffeine right now.

Her chin quivered. "When I got to his apartment, his door was cracked open. He didn't answer, so I went inside. I found him. Dead."

He reserved his opinion on other reasons why the man could have died. Heart attack? Accident? Dead did not mean murdered. "That must have been traumatic for you."

"Not as traumatic as seeing a seafood-flavored potato chips wrapper and an empty energy drink beside him."

Bradley bristled. He didn't think the woman was making much sense, but he knew what she was getting at. Darrell had loved both of those treats, and it was rare to see him without one or the other…or both. Still, he didn't want to jump to conclusions. "What did you do?"

"I got in my car and started driving. I didn't know where to go or what to do. I ended up here."

"Why here? Why me?" Instead of the police? He didn't ask the last question. Not yet, at least.

She rubbed her collarbone and stared at the fire in front of her, as if in another world. "I can't go to the police and tell them that a dead man is trying to kill me. So I have to prove that he's not dead. You're the only person I could think of who could help me with that."

He swallowed, trying to formulate the best response, one that wouldn't set her off in a tirade or into tears. "Two dead men—one supposedly accidental and one supposedly murdered—don't mean your fiancé is alive."

"It's more than that. I can feel him watching me. My gut is telling me that he's still here, that he never died." Her strained gaze met his. "You really do think I'm out of my mind, don't you?"

How did he answer that? Finally, he shook his head. "I think you're scared."

She reached into her back pocket and pulled out a cell phone. The device trembled in her slender hands. "Today I got this."

Bradley took the phone from her and glanced at the text message on the screen. He read the threatening words.

I did it for you.

Then he saw the sender had left his initials: D.L. Darrell Lewis.

Someone was playing with this woman's head. The question was why?

Julianne's gaze locked on Bradley's as desperation for the truth caused adrenaline to surge through her veins. She swallowed, pressure welling in her—pressure not to fail, pressure to put that old part of her life behind her…so she might actually have some hope for her future.

"Do you believe me now?" Someone *had* to believe her.

But she hardly believed herself. Her story was crazy. She could acknowledge that. But her gut told her that something wasn't right, and she didn't have anything—or anyone—else to trust at the moment. She held her breath as she waited for Bradley's response.

Bradley didn't blink, didn't shift even. Instead, he stared back at her, his voice calm and controlled. "You should go to the police, Julianne. They're probably looking for you now, anyway."

Her eyes widened, and she gripped the arm of the chair. "Looking for me? What are you talking about?"

He waited a moment before responding, and

when he finally spoke his words were maddeningly detached. "You fled the scene of a murder. Your fingerprints are probably going to be found there. They'll want to question you."

"But I didn't do anything!" Panic raced through her—again. She stood and began pacing the wood floor, the flames from the fire heating her skin as she strode back and forth.

"I didn't say you did. But that doesn't mean the police won't be looking for you."

She shook her head with more gusto than she thought she could muster. "I can't go back. I can't. But I don't know *what* to do." She let her head drop down toward her chest. In all honesty, she hadn't really thought any of this through. Fear had propelled her to run, and the search for answers had led her here. To a man who didn't believe her.

A tree had more emotions than this stoic giant in front of her.

She brushed off her jeans and pulled herself up to full height. She wouldn't put herself at the mercy of someone who pitied her. She had more self-respect than that. "I appreciate you seeing me. I apologize for wasting your time." She had to get out of here and figure out her plan B. She knew a dead end when she saw one, and Bradley Stone was just that.

She sensed him standing as she walked toward the door.

"What are you going to do now?" His deep voice

reverberated through the room, all the way down to her bones.

She turned toward him. "I'm going to keep looking. I can't stop. I can't live like this anymore." She'd think about the logistics later, things like warmth, food, money and personal safety. She was strong and resilient. Somehow she'd get through this. She ignored the nagging doubts threatening to emerge.

"Good luck." His voice sounded solemn, as if he was speaking to someone facing near certain death.

"Thanks." She was going to need it. "How close is the nearest gas station?"

He tucked a hand into his pocket. "Probably ten, fifteen miles. Why?"

"Because that's where I'm headed." She shivered as she thought about walking that desolate stretch of road again.

He shifted. "That's going to be a long walk."

"I'll be okay." She raised her chin, trying to appear stronger than she felt.

When she got to the door, Bradley called out to her again. "Wait. I'll drive you."

"You don't have to do that." Fear had propelled her to come here, but now she was coming to her senses. This had been a bad idea.

He caught up with her in three strides, and his hand went to her elbow. "Yes, I do."

"I don't want your pity, Commander. I don't want

anyone to placate me. I'll walk to the gas station in the snow if I have to. It beats being ridiculed by a man who thinks he knows everything."

She jerked the door open when Bradley stepped in front of her, his hands raised in peace. "Look, I'm not trying to offend you. Your story is a bit of a stretch, though, even for the most levelheaded person."

He had a point. She couldn't deny that. But that didn't mean she had to put up with Bradley Stone and his infuriating condescension. "I thought you might help, but I was wrong. Now, if you'll excuse me."

He blocked her again. "Don't be so stubborn that you get yourself hurt."

"Darrell is dead. You said so. Therefore, I shouldn't be in danger."

"Darrell or not, someone is threatening you." His eyes softened. "Please, let me drive you to get some gas and then back out to your car. It's the least I can do for the fiancée of one of my guys."

The thought of trekking down the lonely, deserted road as the sun began to sink below the horizon wasn't appealing. In fact, the idea made shivers race across her skin. When she weighed her options—spend time with Bradley Stone or walk the road—the decision was harder than she'd thought it would be. But concern for her safety won out. "If you don't mind, I'll take you up on your offer…and then I'll be out of your hair."

He spread the door open and waited for her to step outside into the frigid day. She should have worn a coat. She should have done a lot of things, but there hadn't been time for that.

Before she realized what was happening, Bradley pulled off his sports jacket and handed it to her. "Put this on."

She rubbed her arms, feeling the goose bumps there. "I'm okay."

"Don't be stubborn. You're obviously cold. Please, wear it."

She didn't feel like arguing anymore, so she took the coat from him and pulled it over her shoulders. The material shielded her from the brisk wind that cut across the lawn, bringing with it a new scent, one that reminded her of a pine forest in the morning.

Bradley's cologne, she realized. The last thing she needed was to be drawn to the scent of someone who was a heartless figure of a man. She shrugged off her thoughts and climbed inside the vehicle. The sun hung low in the distance, temporarily blinding her.

Bradley slid into the driver's seat and started the engine. A moment later, heat blew through the vents. Blessed, glorious heat. Quickly, she tugged off the jacket and placed it in the seat between them. "Thank you," she mumbled, remembering her manners.

He said nothing, stoically putting the vehicle in drive and rolling toward the gate. The guard waved him through, and then silence pulled tight between them. What did Julianne expect? That they'd chat like old friends? Besides, what was there to talk about? The weather? Football? National security?

"How'd you know I worked at Eyes?" Bradley's deep voice snapped her from her thoughts.

"I got a letter from Dawn Turner. It was an update on what everyone from the old team was doing now."

"A letter…?"

"You didn't get one?"

He shook his head. "No, I didn't. It actually said I was working at Eyes now? That isn't exactly public information."

Julianne shrugged. "I have no idea. I just remembered that tidbit of information. So when I started wondering if Darrell was alive, I thought of you. At first, I thought maybe I'd find you so you could confirm he was dead. Then I decided I'd find you to prove that he might be alive."

"I know it's not what you want to hear, Julianne, but there's no way he could have survived that explosion. He was a smart man. He was brazen, sometimes to the point of stupidity. But he was a good SEAL."

The man had loved his job, worshipped it practically. Which made sense, since Darrell had an obsessive personality. The man had no fear, he didn't care what people thought of him and he had a mean determination once he set his mind to something.

Had he set his mind to killing her? If so, why?

She cleared her throat. "A good SEAL or a loose cannon?"

"Depends on who you ask."

"I'm asking you."

Bradley shifted, ever so slightly. "He could be a hotshot sometimes. I like to think he would have gotten that out of his system with a little more maturity."

"You don't strike me as an optimist."

He stared straight ahead. "No offense, but you don't know me."

Nope, she didn't. And she didn't want to. In her opinion, life was too short to be around people who pitied her or treated her like she was beneath them.

Her silver sedan came into sight down the road. She squinted as they got closer. Something looked off, even from the distance. But what?

"Is that yours?" Bradley asked.

"It is." So what if the compact sedan was ten years old? It was paid for, and it got great mileage… unless she took an unexpected trip with no prior planning. She'd been so preoccupied with getting here that she didn't stop for the entire trip—not to eat, to use the bathroom or to even get gas. She'd been single-minded in her mission. Add fear into the mix, and she hadn't even thought to look at the gas gauge. She'd just driven, fast and hard.

Bradley slowed to weave around her car. She sucked in a deep breath as she got a glance of her vehicle, which she'd abandoned on the road since there was no shoulder here. Bradley braked beside it.

All of the windows were busted out. A dent on the hood made Julianne envision someone standing there as they pounded viciously at her car. Papers from the backseat fluttered in the wind.

Her gaze focused on something at the front of the car. There, in the passenger seat, lay a bag of potato chips and an empty energy drink container.

Bradley threw the vehicle into Park and opened his door. He looked back at Julianne and held up a finger. "Stay here."

Julianne didn't say anything, but that same dazed look—one that was full of fear and trepidation—settled over her.

"Julianne?"

She finally made eye contact with him and nodded. Good. She'd heard him and understood.

He locked the door and exited the vehicle. He wished he had his gun with him, but he hadn't planned on leaving the office today. He definitely hadn't planned on this.

He approached the car with caution, his gaze searching his surroundings for any sign of danger. Something about the situation felt off, and he didn't like it.

How long had Julianne been away from the vehicle? Based on the time of the phone call from the guard until now, she could have only been away for an hour and a half max. Had someone been following her? If so, where were they now?

This road led only one place—the Eyes headquarters.

He didn't like the knot in his gut. He'd been in enough life-threatening situations to know when danger lurked nearby. His senses were heightened now.

Then another thought slammed into his mind: What if Julianne was the dangerous one? What if she'd busted these windows out herself in order to make him think something was going on? To make him believe her? What if she really was crazy?

Sure, she was beautiful. Her stunning good looks would blind most people. But Bradley knew better than to be deceived by a person's appearance.

He glanced back at her. Her face was pale, her eyes glazed and her limbs continued to shake. She looked genuinely scared. Could someone fake that? Or perhaps she was scared of herself?

The question was what did he do with her now? How did he sort this out?

He had a million other things to do. Helping a potentially unbalanced woman wasn't on his agenda, nor could he squeeze one more thing onto his schedule.

But, at the same time, how could he turn her away? If she did have some scheme up her sleeve, perhaps he should keep her close to keep an eye on her. He sighed and climbed back into the SUV.

Julianne's gaze latched onto his. "Well?"

He had to decide on his plan of action, decide whether he should walk away or engage himself. "Is there anyone you can call?"

"My boss is dead. My counselor is dead. My best friend just moved to California, and my parents are backpacking in Europe." She shook her head, rubbing her lips together as she did so. "Look, I'll just call a tow truck and get my car taken into a repair shop."

He quirked a brow. "And then what?"

"What do you mean?"

"What will you do after that?" he asked.

Julianne glanced down at her hands, continuing to shake her head and rub her lips. "I have no idea. I can't go back up to my apartment. I don't have enough money to go anywhere else." She shrugged. "How hard could it be to go somewhere and start a new life? Get a new job, find a cheap apartment, pay in cash. I'll do whatever it takes to make sure Darrell doesn't find me again."

The woman was serious. Getting her car fixed was going to drain most of her money, he would guess. She didn't seem like the type who kept a large stash of cash on hand. Starting over wasn't as easy as the woman might think.

"I hope you brought enough money for all of that."

She grimaced. "I have forty-two dollars in cash. I don't use credit cards, and my checking account has twelve dollars left. I don't know what I'm going to do or how I'm going to do it, but I'll figure it out. What choice do I have?"

"Come back to Eyes, and we'll call that tow truck." It would take probably a day, at least, to fix the car. Which meant she'd have to find a hotel overnight. Except that she probably couldn't afford a hotel.

The last thing he wanted was to add more stress to his life. So why was he even considering helping her out? Because he probably wasn't much different than Eric, the guard stationed at the gate. A beautiful woman who needed help was hard to resist.

"I'm sorry to inconvenience you like this." She ran a hand through her hair, rumpling the golden-brown waves that cascaded down her shoulders.

"Don't worry about it. I can reschedule the meetings on my calendar." Just not the one next week with the Department of Defense. He couldn't lose that contract. He'd been working toward it for the past nine months.

He pulled forward, looking for a place to turn around.

That's when he heard a pop. The back window shattered.

"Get down!" He pushed Julianne to the floor as he swerved the SUV around, barely avoiding the ditch on the other side of the road.

Another bullet exploded against the passenger window. Shards of glass rained to the floor.

Just what was going on? He prayed that God would shield them from the danger that was closing in.

THREE

The fear that coursed through Julianne made her powerless to scream, to move. Thankfully, Bradley had pushed her to the floor. If not, she would have been an easy target as she'd sat frozen in the passenger seat.

Would Bradley believe her now?

How could he not?

Her heart pounded in her ears, each beat quick and frantic.

She'd thought the nightmare of Darrell was over when he died. Maybe it was just beginning, though. Maybe the terror she'd felt when they'd dated was just a prelude of even worse things to come.

"Is there anything you're not telling me, Julianne?" Bradley's grip was tight on the steering wheel as he swerved to right the vehicle after the bullets had assailed them. He accelerated, flying down the road with so much speed that a wave of nausea rose to her throat. "What do you mean?"

"Who's shooting at us?" he demanded.

"I told you. Darrell Lewis."

"Darrell is dead."

"Then I have no idea." She came to her senses enough to hold her hands over her head as bits of glass continued to shower down over her. "Do you believe me now that something is going on?"

"I believe *something* is going on."

What did that mean? Was he implying that she actually had something to do with this? Why would she?

The vehicle slowed as distance stretched between them and the shooter. But the intensity didn't leave Bradley's gaze, didn't slacken his grip on the wheel or the set of his shoulders.

Julianne pulled herself up from the floor, pieces of glass falling from her hair and clinking against the leather upholstered seat. Her elbow throbbed; she vaguely remembered jamming it on the console on her way down. It didn't seem important at the time—staying alive did. Now she realized she'd have a nice bruise there to remind her of today's events. She'd take a bruise over the alternatives— which included death.

"You okay?"

She nodded. "I guess."

They pulled up to the Eyes headquarters, and Julianne could tell that Bradley stewed over the situation. She let him, sensing he needed space to sort out his thoughts.

When she got out of the car, she wished she still had Bradley's jacket and that she wasn't so stubborn. If she wore it now, however, she'd feel like a traitor. She wasn't sure if he was a friend or foe— but the majority of times since she'd encountered him, he felt like an enemy.

He ushered her inside, then paused at the stairway and pulled out his phone. Who could he possibly be calling right now? Maybe he was turning her in? Maybe he thought this whole situation was her doing? She had no clue.

She wandered to the fireplace. What now? No car. No money. No friends.

Lord, you've always taken care of me, but even I can't see a way out of this situation. What am I going to do?

God concerned himself with the lilies of the field. Certainly, he'd concern himself with her also. She was simply at the point where how that would play out seemed unfathomable.

A man in uniform came down the stairs and stopped beside Bradley. He greeted the newcomer and pointed to her. "Julianne, I need you to stay with Wayne while I take care of some business."

"Is he my babysitter?" she asked, indignation creeping up her spine.

Bradley shifted, almost appearing like a disgruntled father figure. "No, not a babysitter. But you don't have the clearance to be here. I need to call a tow truck and settle some other business. Wayne here will take you to get some food and make sure you're comfortable for a few minutes while I get my affairs in order."

Guilt rushed through her. She shouldn't have been so quick to judge. He was just trying to help her, she chided herself. When would she ever be able to trust another man?

Never, she thought.

Not after all the abuse she'd endured at the hands of her fiancé. As much as she'd hoped and prayed to one day get past all this, now she knew that she simply needed to find contentment in being single—forever.

She nodded and licked her lips as he walked away. Her temporary guard led her to the cafeteria. Her stomach rumbled. She hadn't eaten yet today. She had some leftover pasta in the fridge at her apartment that she'd planned on heating up.

Wasn't that her life most days? Cook for herself. Work by herself. Counsel others on the emergency hotline while never applying her own advice?

She'd made some effort to merge into the social scene again. She'd begun to see a counselor to get over her paralyzing fears—but then he'd died in the auto accident. She'd gone into the office three days a week and worked at home the other two. Once a month, she traveled to visit her parents, and on Sundays she went to church. Mostly, she liked to stay in by herself, though. The confines of her apartment felt safe.

She knew this was no way to live and that she shouldn't let one person dictate her fears...but how could she forget? The scar across her collarbone reminded her every day about the damage another person was capable of inflicting—and that was just the physical damage. The emotional damage...well, that went deeper than any scar tissue could.

She picked up a sandwich, some fruit and a bottle of water. As she sat at the table and stared out the window, her appetite vanished and worry set in once again.

She would get through this, she reminded herself. She'd find a way.

After all, nothing was impossible with God.

But, right now, the impossible seemed to be staring her in the face.

Bradley needed to tell his boss, Jack Sergeant, about what was going on, especially since Julianne Grace had showed up here right when they were on the cusp of signing a huge contract with the Department of Defense. He also needed a moment away from Julianne and her whirlwind story. How had today turned into such a circus? He caught Jack in his office and gave him the detailed version of events.

"What do you know about the woman?" Jack

crossed his arms and leaned against his desk. He was a tall, broad man in his early thirties who had perceptive eyes and a head full of close-cropped dark hair. He was also one of the toughest soldiers Bradley had ever met.

Bradley sat down in the chair across from him, his head still spinning. He rubbed his chin thoughtfully before shaking his head. "Not much. Just that she was engaged to one of my men back when I was a SEAL. I haven't seen her in two years, and then she showed up here today out of the blue."

"What about this guy she was engaged to?" Jack asked. "Tell me about him."

"He was brazen, smart, a little headstrong." Bradley shook his head again. "I don't know. I always wondered if there was something a little off about him. But people say you have to be a little crazy to be a SEAL. He passed all of the physical and psychological tests—you know how hard that is." Jack had been a SEAL also, but he'd never worked with Darrell.

His boss's hands went to his hips. "Even if she set up the car herself to make it look like something happened, there's no way she could have fired the shots at herself."

Bradley had thought of that. "But a dead fiancé couldn't have fired them, either."

"Are you sure he's dead?" In typical Jack fashion, the man didn't even blink as he waited.

"If he staged his own death, then he's brilliant. The explosion happened, and I was on the scene two minutes later. I don't see any way it couldn't have been Darrell, not to mention that the autopsy confirmed it." Bradley ran a hand over his jaw. "Terror groups have had us in their sights with this new contract on the horizon. Maybe someone is paying off Julianne, using her as a decoy to distract us."

"What are you going to do, then?"

That was the question of the hour. "I can't exactly send her on her way. She has no car, no money and nowhere to turn."

"If she is a decoy, maybe we should keep our eye on her."

Just then Bradley's cell phone rang. He recognized the number's prefix as the local police department. He furrowed his brows before answering, instantly on guard for whatever this conversation might hold.

"Is this Bradley Stone?" a man asked.

He tensed. "Yes, it is."

"Mr. Stone, this is Virginia Beach police detective Arnold Spencer. Did you have a car towed to First Class Auto on Princess Anne Road today?"

"I did." He blew out a breath, not liking where this conversation was going.

"We need you to come down to the station so we can ask you a few questions."

Ask him a few questions? Why? Just what had he gotten himself mixed up in? "Questions pertaining to what?"

"When the mechanic started the engine, the car burst into flames. One man is in critical condition and two others are injured."

Bradley closed his eyes. The car exploded? Was Julianne the intended target? Or had she lured him to the scene, hoping he'd be the next victim?

Julianne sat in the same chair by the fireplace, finding comfort in the familiar—though it had only been familiar for the past couple of hours. But she'd take whatever she could get. Wayne stood a respectful distance away, subtly alert to everything around him.

What was Bradley doing? Calling the police to come take her away? Certainly he couldn't still be skeptical. After all, she couldn't have fired that gun at herself.

But Bradley was unreadable. How ironic that her only shot at finding answers was in the form of a cold, heartless man who only cared about his career. She'd been shocked to learn he'd even gotten out of the navy. He seemed like the career military type.

Just then, Julianne heard someone stomping down the stairs. She looked up and saw Bradley. The scowl on his face told her that something was

wrong. What now? Had he found something else
out and changed his mind about helping her? She
sighed with frustration. Why had she turned to
this man in the first place? He'd hardly ever spoken to her.

But Darrell had always held him in such high re-
gard. And, even though her fiancé lacked character,
he seemed to know a good thing when he had it.
He'd talked about how Bradley would risk his life
for others. How he was tough but fair. How he'd
climbed his way to the top, despite his hard child-
hood. He'd proven that you could be anything you
wanted to be.

That's what Darrell had said.

At the time, Julianne had dismissed the praise.
She'd had other things to worry about—like how
to break up with Darrell and survive.

But after the events of the past couple of months,
Bradley's face had continually popped into her
mind.

And almost every time it did, the man was scowling, just like he was right now. She stood, wiping
any crumbs from her pants and hoping there were
none on her face, for that matter.

"Commander." She nodded.

"Just call me Bradley." He stopped in front of her,
paused and then shifted. The motion only lasted
three seconds, but those three seconds were long
enough to put Julianne on edge. He was going to

tell her something—something that wasn't good. She could sense it, and her muscles tensed as she waited. "You need to come with me down to the police station."

The anxiety fluttering through her body intensified. Was he turning her in? What was she guilty of? Her gaze shifted around her. Could she run? No, there were too many people around to stop her. She was going to have to face this head on. Her gaze met Bradley's again. "What's going on?"

He stared at her, watching her reaction a little too closely. "Your car. It exploded when the mechanic started the engine."

The color drained from her face. Why did things keep going from bad to worse? "My car exploded? How did that happen?"

"I'm hoping you can tell me." Something in his gaze seemed to scream accusation.

She jammed her finger into her chest. "Me? What are you talking about? Why would I be able to tell you that?" The truth hit her, and blood rushed through her veins. "You think I did this? But that makes no sense. Why would I rig my own car?"

"No one said you did that." His expression remained neutral, which made Julianne want to reach up and shake him until his real feelings came to the surface.

Instead, she shoved her hands into her pockets,

just to make sure she didn't do anything she'd regret. "You certainly implied it."

He shifted again, his cold blue eyes never leaving hers. "Look, we're working on developing some products that the enemy would love to get their hands on. We don't rule anything out as a coincidence. You showing up here. Today. And with this crazy story…It would make anyone suspicious."

She sucked in a deep breath, trying to think with a clear head. Impossible. Bradley lowered himself into a chair across from her, his eyes on her. They'd softened—just slightly. But she wasn't sure if his gaze held compassion or pity. She didn't want anyone's pity; she knew that. "I don't know what to say," she finally muttered.

Bradley leaned toward her, his voice low. "Julianne, is someone making you do this?"

His words settled over her and, as his insinuations hit home, agitation ricocheted through her. "Making me do this? Are you serious? You think someone has a gun to my head, telling me to distract you from the task at hand…or they'll kill me? Is that what you're saying?"

"The thought did run through my head." His voice remained even and steady, which only increased her agitation.

"Well, you're the crazy one if you think I would do that." Her voice rose in pitch, cracking every other syllable as emotions rose to the surface. "I came here because I thought I could trust you. I was wrong."

She stood and stormed toward the door. Where she thought she was going, she had no idea. She had no car and, even if she started walking, she had nowhere to go. She just knew that she couldn't stand here and be insulted.

"Julianne—" Bradley called her name, his voice softer than before.

She pretended not to hear him and continued marching forward, trying to draw back the tears that wanted to flood down her cheeks.

Tears showed weakness…and the last thing she wanted was to appear weak in front of the stone-cold commander.

Before she got to the door, a strong hand wrapped around her arm—not too hard, but hard enough that she stopped. "Wait. You can't go."

She jerked out of his grasp. "Watch me."

"No, really, you can't go. I promised the detective I'd take you down to the station."

And for a moment she'd thought he was just being nice. She should have known better. His words echoed in her mind. *I promised the detective I'd take you down to the station.*

She stared at him accusingly. "So you're actually going to march me down to the police station so they can arrest me? Well, I guess that shouldn't surprise me. After all, you're probably the one who told them that I most likely set that bomb up myself, hoping it would detonate when you got behind the wheel." She frowned. "What sense does that make? If I wanted you to do that, why would I have busted out the windows? And who was in the woods shooting at us?"

"I understand that none of this makes sense. We just want some answers."

She jammed her finger into her chest again. "*I* want some answers. That's why I came here."

"Why don't we sort this out down at the station?"

She crossed her arms, hating herself for feeling so immature. "Fine."

"Let's go." He gripped her arm and he steered her out the door and back into a different SUV—this one without bullet holes. She hardly knew what to say or what to think. Her mind whirled over the revelations as she pulled her seat belt across her shoulder and waist.

She still couldn't believe her car had exploded. Had Darrell set that up after her car ran out of gas? It seemed unlikely. He would have had to be watching her all day—known that she'd discovered her boss's body, known that she might run. Then he would have had to follow her and wait for just the right opportunity to rig her car.

Unlikely, but possible.

Darrell had been an "ultra-prepared" kind of

guy. What if now he was ultra-prepared to stage an accident, to put others' lives in danger?

Had the bomb been intended for her? Had he hoped to finally accomplish his original mission—that if he couldn't have her, he'd make sure no one wanted her? Nothing made sense.

"What are you thinking?" Bradley asked as they began down the road.

"Why do you care?" There she went again, sounding like a brat. But how was she supposed to act when the man thought she could either be a criminal...or was being manipulated by a criminal?

With love, that was how.

Wasn't that what the Bible taught? And didn't she try to live by the Bible's commands?

"I know I could have reacted better, but you've got to understand where I'm coming from. The timing of you being here is uncanny. Your story is...unexpected."

He was being nice. And he had a point. If she put herself in his shoes, she could understand why her appearance had him off kilter. "I get it."

"I don't think you do. I don't think you realize the scope of the project we're working on. We're on the precipice of some new technology that could revolutionize warfare as we know it. It will keep our soldiers safe. Safe is not what the enemy wants."

Her throat burned. "You're right...it's not. But I assure you, my allegiance is to this country and not to the enemy. I even thought briefly after high school about joining the military myself."

"Why didn't you?"

"I'm not exactly the commando type. My heart was really for helping the hurting, so I studied social work and counseling instead."

"Noble callings within themselves."

"I like it. I like helping others make sense of their emotions and their circumstances." If only it were that easy to make sense of her own tumultuous life.

Alan had been trying to help her do that. She'd realized that she needed to deal with the effects of her relationship with Darrell. She'd tried to handle the fallout on her own but had done a lousy job with it. She still had nightmares. She still checked behind corners. She had trouble getting close to people.

She hadn't always been like this. There was a time in her life that she'd loved being around people, that she'd loved immersing herself in life. But lately she'd found herself withdrawing into her own little cave and shutting people out.

She knew something had to change. She had no desire to live the rest of her life like this. She'd just started making some progress with Alan when… She shook her head. She couldn't think about it.

Not now. There were so many other things to think about. None of them, however, were things

she wanted to ponder. As they cruised toward the
police station, she realized she had no choice in
the matter.

FOUR

Bradley leaned against the reception desk at the police precinct. "We're here to see Detective Spencer."

The receptionist promised him that the detective would be right down.

Bradley glanced at Julianne as he went to sit in the plastic chair beside her. Her hazel eyes almost looked frantic. He wasn't sure if the emotion was because she had instigated the craziness or been the recipient of the craziness around them, though.

They waited, the minutes ticking by painfully slow. He could only imagine what might be running through the woman's mind. She was scared… and she should be. Whatever was happening—and whatever side of it she found herself on—the danger was apparent.

A thirtysomething man with a receding hairline and round face stepped into the waiting area and introduced himself as Detective Spencer. Bradley kept a hand at her elbow as they followed him to his office. He wasn't sure if the contact was to keep her standing or to make sure she didn't run. Either way, his hand remained there, despite Julianne's resistance to it. Yes, he'd noticed the way she tried to pull away, to nudge his hand off. He didn't allow it.

In his gut, Bradley knew he wanted to believe Julianne. He didn't know why, but he did. Maybe it was her wide, luminous eyes. Or her quivering voice. Or the sweet scene of daisies on a rainy day that drifted from her flowing hair.

Daisies on a rainy day? What had gotten into him? He sounded like a sap.

He was good at reading people. It had helped him survive. But right now he didn't know if he was reading Julianne correctly, or if he was letting his heart get in the way.

Either way, he had to stay on guard.

He thought briefly about leaving Julianne here at the station and letting the police deal with her. But he couldn't do that. He didn't know what was going on or how Julianne was involved, but he did know that the woman needed someone right now. She looked as if she needed a good meal, a winter coat and a hug, too, for that matter.

Detective Spencer led them to a tiny office, making small talk along the way. Once inside the office, Julianne sat in a chair across from the detective's desk. Bradley decided to stand behind her.

As the detective prodded, Julianne relayed the

same story she'd told Bradley earlier. The detective took notes. Bradley watched as his eyes flickered in doubt as she mentioned the possibility of her fiancé still being alive and behind the attacks.

She finished and stared at the detective a moment. She licked her lips before whispering, "He... he wasn't a nice man."

What did that mean? What had Darrell done to her? Had he simply been rude and self-centered? Or did his abrasiveness come out in other ways—more damaging ways?

Anger simmered in Bradley at the thought. He'd seen his dad hit his mother on more than one occasion. Mostly she'd taken the hits so that Bradley wouldn't have to. He'd been shipped off to foster care and, while there, his parents had both died in a house fire. All the evidence seemed to point to a cigarette igniting the bed in the master bedroom.

Later, at thirteen, Bradley had moved across country to live with an uncle he'd never met. It had taken time to adjust to the new family and the vast contrast between his old life and his new. But his Uncle Bill and Aunt Jackie had proven to be a great blessing in his life, showing him what love really looked like and teaching him about living out the Great Commission. His uncle had also been a SEAL and later a defense contractor. It was his influence that had led Bradley to where he was today. He still missed his uncle, who'd died three years ago from cancer.

Detective Spencer closed his notebook. "Ms. Grace, I've put in a call to the police up in Arlington about your boss and his supposed murder. I'll need you to stay in town in case we have any more questions."

Julianne swallowed hard. Bradley could see the action from his stance behind her, see how she tried to compose herself before nodding.

She had to stay in town. Jack had mentioned that maybe they should keep an eye on her—whether she was on their side or not. How would they do that? Where would she stay while she was in town?

There was a women's shelter that one of his friends from church ran. Maybe Julianne could stay there for the night. Maybe he should just give her some money for a hotel.

Then he remembered the smashed car windows. The gunshots. The report of her car exploding.

He remembered the look of terror in her eyes, the tremble of her hands, the strain in her voice.

He didn't intend for the words to leave his mouth, but he found himself saying, "I'll make sure she sticks around." He was getting in deeper than he intended to. Way deeper.

But he thought about what the Bible said about the least of these. If he didn't help someone who needed help, was he any better than the rest of the world? And wasn't he called to be set apart?

Julianne stood as Detective Spencer dismissed them. She paused in the doorway and dragged her eyes back to the detective. "How's the mechanic doing?"

"He's in critical condition. The explosion could have easily killed him. It's a near miracle he's alive. The shop is condemned, and two others employees had minor cuts and bruises. Overall, it could have been much worse, though."

Her hand slipped over her mouth, probably to cover the O of horror that her lips formed. He didn't need to be a detective to know that reality was hitting her hard. That Julianne could have easily died. Did someone who was working for the other side show that much concern about the people who'd been injured in the battle? He didn't think so.

Just then, something buzzed in her pocket. With shaky hands, she pulled out her cell phone and flipped it open. She closed her eyes after reading something there.

"What?" Bradley stepped closer.

She said nothing, just handed him the phone. He read the words there.

Don't make me keep doing this. It's all in the name of love. With my utmost affection, Your One and Only.

Bradley looked at Julianne, and she nodded at his silent question.

The text message was from Darrell—or someone masquerading as Darrell.

Bradley drew in a long deep breath, realizing that he wouldn't be able to live with himself if he didn't get to the bottom of this—and help Julianne.

Julianne stared blankly at the landscape as they rolled down the road.

Darrell still had the ability to manipulate her emotions as if they were putty. Guilt flooded through her. Though she knew on a logical level that nothing that had happened was her fault, her emotions swerved wildly between guilt and anger, apprehension and sorrow.

Bradley said very little beside her, and that was fine. She didn't bother to ask where he was taking her. If worse had come to worst, she thought she could at least spend the night in her car. Now that wasn't even an option.

But she wasn't going to feel despair. She wasn't going to let Darrell win.

Despite that, another tear rolled down her cheek. When would all of her emotion dry up? Why did she have to feel so weak?

She turned more fully toward the window, not wanting Bradley to see her. She blinked several times, trying to get her vision to clear. Finally, she saw sandy dunes and beach houses perched high on stilts. Beyond them, the ocean collided with the shore, the sand empty of its summertime visitors.

She still said nothing, asked nothing. What good would it do? They'd get to their destination, Bradley would drop her off and she'd figure out what to do.

Except that he'd promised to keep an eye on her. Just how did he plan on doing that?

The car stopped at an oceanfront house. Julianne soaked in the grand structure. Three levels. Mostly windows on the side facing the ocean. An interesting design with lots of angles and recesses and details. White-trimmed decks jutted out from the second and third levels. Neatly kept live oak trees surrounded the perimeters.

When he cut the engine, Julianne dared to look at him. "Where are we?"

He pointed to a door on the first level of the home. "There's a small apartment there. Nothing fancy, just a living room with a pullout couch, a kitchen and a bathroom. You can stay there until this mess clears up."

"Is this…yours?" Just how much did they pay the man to work at Eyes? This home had to cost close to a million.

"It is. It used to be a rental property. The original owner kept an apartment on the bottom level so he could keep an eye on the place." He climbed out, and Julianne followed suite. As soon as she stepped out, the breeze coming off the ocean assaulted her already-frigid skin.

She shivered before stepping around the corner and spotting the glorious blue of the ocean. For a moment, she forgot about the cold and was swept away by the water's vastness. "It's beautiful."

"I like it."

She scrambled behind him as he strode toward the apartment. He jammed a key into the lock and pushed open the door. At his insistence, she slipped inside, quickly glancing around at the minimal decorations and furnishings of the space. Not that she was complaining.

She looked back at Bradley, who stood in the doorway, allowing a biting wind to sweep over the tile floor. She cleared her throat, trying to remember her manners. "I really appreciate this, Command—Bradley, I mean. I know you don't have to do this. I promise you, I won't make you regret it. You'll see."

The look in his eyes showed doubt. Instead of acknowledging her gratitude, he pushed a key into her hand. "I'll be working upstairs. If you need anything, don't hesitate to let me know."

After he disappeared, Julianne stared at the apartment around her, a place in desperate need of a woman's touch. Everything was purely functional with no personality whatsoever. She found the thermostat and cranked the heat, which contradicted her need to open the windows and air the space out. Comfort won out over the stale smell, though.

How had she gotten here? And what exactly was she going to do now?

Right now, she decided, she needed to take some safety precautions. If Darrell was alive and if he'd followed her this far, why would he stop now? The apartment had six windows—three in the back and three in the front, plus the door. She checked the locks on each of the windows and tugged at the doorknob to make sure it was secure.

When that was done, she sat back on the couch. The sun had almost completely disappeared from the sky, but she had no toothbrush or pajamas. She had no food, even, and no car that would allow her to drive and get some supplies. The last thing she wanted to do was to bother Bradley. The man, in one sense, had gone out of his way to help her. In another way, he seemed reluctant to have anything to do with her. She couldn't quite figure him out.

And she wouldn't try to. No, hopefully she'd be gone before she had a chance to try to do that.

What a predicament. She sighed and let her head fall back against the couch cushions. At least she was alive. And, for the moment, she felt safe. She'd checked the mirrors on her way here and hadn't seen anyone following. Of course, she'd never seen anyone following her before but someone had always been there.

The ocean seemed to beckon her. Despite her desire to hunker down for the evening, she wrapped a blanket around herself and ventured outside toward the beach. As long as she didn't wander too far away, she'd be okay. Besides, she hadn't seen anyone following them. Maybe she still had a day or two before Darrell found her again, so she might as well enjoy the view now.

Though the sunset to the west, its colors smeared across the horizon of the Atlantic. She plopped down on a sand dune and absorbed life around her. The waves crashed on the shore, churning with angry force today. Seagulls swooped toward the sand, trying to find any stray food. Otherwise, the beach was empty. Everyone else knew better than to be out in this cold.

She shivered, despite her blanket. She felt so alone in the world, felt so much as if something could happen to her and no one would care. Sure, her parents would care but they were off living the young adulthood they never got to experience because they'd found out they were pregnant with her. Her best friend had moved away and had a new life. The only two other people in her life were now dead.

She shivered again, halfway from the cold and halfway from the chill of loneliness.

Lord, will the ache in my soul ever go away?

"Hi there," a soft voice said behind her.

Julianne flinched and turned toward the sound. The crashing of the waves had obscured the sound of any car doors slamming. She needed to remember that—and remember not to get too wrapped up in the moment.

A striking brunette walked off the dunes toward her, a welcoming smile on her face as she extended her hand. "I didn't mean to scare you. I'm Elle Philips...a friend of Bradley's."

A friend? Was this his girlfriend? Julianne glanced at her finger and saw the engagement ring there. She seemed like the type of woman Bradley would go for—beautiful, classy, stable.

Elle settled beside her on the dune. "Bradley told me what happened and I brought you a few things. I'm a little shorter than you, but I'm hoping the clothes will fit. I put in a few other things that you might need, as well."

Julianne's heart swelled with gratitude. "Thank you. I appreciate that."

"I can't stay long because I have a board meeting tonight. But Bradley told me a little about what was going on. I've been through some tough situations, and I know how easy it is to feel like you're losing your sanity. If you need anything, you can always call me."

"I appreciate that...more than you know. I feel

badly that I'm putting Bradley out, but I'm out of options."

Elle pushed a hair behind her ear, her expression earnest and confident as she nodded. "Bradley's a good guy. Don't let his gruff side fool you. He's actually one of the nicest men you'll ever meet."

Julianne couldn't help but point to her ring. "When's the wedding?"

Elle glanced at the ring and her face morphed from surprise to amusement. "Oh, no. I'm not engaged to Bradley. But I am getting married to a great guy in another month. Bradley...well, Bradley will probably never get married." She sighed sadly. "His fiancée, Vanessa, died a year ago, and he's retreated into a shell since then. We're still holding out hope that he'll come out of it."

His fiancée had died? Julianne's heart twisted. For most people, the death of a fiancée would be one of the worst things that could happen to them. People had thought that of her when Darrell supposedly died. They'd thought she'd mourned the loss of their future together. If she'd truly been happy and in love, then his death would have been horrible. Instead, his death was a relief.

She wondered exactly what had happened with Bradley's fiancée. She couldn't bring herself to ask because it wasn't her business, and she knew that.

Elle nodded behind her. "Bradley's at the window now, probably wishing you weren't out here."

Julianne glanced behind her and saw his silhouette there, watching them. "I should probably get back to the apartment. I just couldn't stay away from the ocean. It makes your problems seem small, doesn't it?"

"Absolutely." Elle stood and wiped the sand from her jeans. "Listen, I left a few groceries on your doorstep, too. You're in good hands with Bradley. He's tough and he's got integrity."

Julianne was grateful for the reassurance. She walked with Elle back toward the house, helped her carry in the four bags she'd brought, and said goodbye.

Then she sat alone in her apartment with only her thoughts for company.

Unfortunately, her thoughts were the last thing she wanted to be alone with right now.

Some of the tension left Bradley's chest as Julianne and Elle walked away from the shore. He didn't want to try to control the woman, but he certainly didn't think it was a good idea for her to be on the shore, not when he considered everything that had happened. He'd watched behind them as they'd driven back to his house, and he'd seen no sign of anything suspicious. Maybe she'd be safe here...for a few days, at least.

He was grateful that Elle had offered to bring some things over for her because, out of all the things he was good at, picking out clothes and other necessities for a woman was not one of them. Elle was engaged to one of his best friends, Mark Denton, and her thoughtfulness never ceased to amaze him. She and Mark would be happy together.

He'd thought he'd live out the rest of his life with the woman of his dreams, also. But while his fiancée, Vanessa, was house sitting for him when he was away on business, someone had broken into his home. When the intruder had run into her, he'd pulled the trigger. One shot in the head, and her life on this earth was gone. His dreams, their hopes together, all of their plans—disappeared forever.

The police had never caught the person behind her murder, and every night when Bradley lay down to try to sleep, he thought about her death. He thought about ways to track down her killer. But so far, all of them had turned up empty. Nothing had been taken from his apartment. No evidence, other than the bullet, had been left. It was almost as if a ghost had appeared, ruined his life and then disappeared along with his dreams.

He turned from the window and thought about making something to eat—or even ordering something to eat—and inviting Julianne to join him, but he just couldn't bring himself to do it. He'd do what he could to help her, but he'd keep his distance. Even if the woman could be trusted, getting close to her wouldn't do anyone any good.

He continued to work in his office, making himself a sandwich to eat at his desk. His thoughts drifted back to Julianne, though. Just what was she doing downstairs? Was she okay?

Finally, well after the sun went down and darkness had fallen, he set the alarm—sure it would go off if Julianne opened the door, but that could work in his favor—and turned in for the night. The clock beside his bed read eleven-thirty, and sleep wouldn't find him. Instead, he walked to the window and peered outside.

That's when he saw a shadow duck behind his car.

He tensed, watching. The shadow appeared again, moving toward the house.

He grabbed his gun and ran toward the door, determined to find some answers once and for all.

FIVE

Harsh pounding sounded outside of Julianne's apartment. Each hit seemed to pull her nerves tighter and tighter. Her first instinct was to draw the covers up and let fear take over. A close second was to hide in the closet and pray that no one would break down the door. But she couldn't do either of those things. She'd just be a sitting duck if she did.

The pounding became louder, more urgent. Was someone trying to get inside her house? Who? Why?

She swallowed and resolutely threw off the covers around her. Her gaze roamed the room. She needed a weapon. Something. Anything. Her scan stopped at a lamp on the table beside her bed. She unplugged the heavy iron piece, wrapped her hands around the narrowest section and held it like a baseball bat as she started toward the door.

Her heart thudded in her ears. What was she doing? Did she really think she could conquer her fears with a lamp? Despite her doubts, she sucked in a breath and continued taking baby steps toward the sound.

Could it be Darrell making all that noise? He wasn't the type to knock and announce his presence in a shock and awe type of tactic. No, he was the type to sneak in and surprise her unaware. Guerrilla warfare, as they'd say in the military.

"Julianne, are you all right?" A gruff voice cut into the night.

Bradley, Julianne realized, her heart rate slowing. Was that Bradley at the door? What was going on?

Lowering the lamp, she hurried across the room and unlatched the three locks. Bradley stood outside wearing sweats, a T-shirt and wielding a gun. His gaze was fierce and his stance rigid. Something about seeing him there got Julianne's pulse racing. No, not seeing him. It was the situation, the danger that caused adrenaline to pump through her, not the handsome man standing outside the door.

She cleared her throat and looped a piece of hair behind her ear. "I'm here."

His gaze seemed to absorb her, the intensity of the scrutiny causing her to blush. "I saw someone outside. Did you see anything? Hear anything?"

She shook her head, fear spreading through her. "Nothing. Just you."

He offered a crisp nod. "Stay put. And call the police if I don't return within the hour."

"If you don't…?" She shut her mouth and nodded, not wanting to think about the implications of what he was saying. "Okay."

She closed the door and turned the locks, checking each latch twice. Three times, for that matter. Then she backed away from the door. She kept backing up until she hit a wall. She stood there, frozen to the spot, her eyes darting around from one window to the next. She expected to see shadows, to hear yells and footfalls, to flinch from the sound of gunshots.

Instead, she heard nothing.

Was Darrell out there? Had he found her? What about Bradley? Was he hurt?

The room suddenly felt ice-cold. The plaster against her back seeped through her clothing and chilled her skin. Everything in the apartment seemed to hold its breath with her. Not a sound escaped from anywhere. But the silence held its own fear as questions without answers hung suspended in the air.

A shadow passed the window, creeping toward the door.

She gulped down a breath, fighting panic. Bradley? Or Darrell?

Her fingers scratched the wall. She should have called the police. Should have grabbed the phone, at least. Instead, she'd frozen. The ice around her limbs refused to give.

A bang shook the entire room. "Julianne, it's me. Bradley. Open up."

She inhaled, realizing that she'd stopped breathing out of anticipation. She propelled herself from the wall and across the room. Her fingers shook so badly that she didn't think she'd get the locks turned. But finally she did. She cracked the door open, suspicion still lingering in her mind.

Bradley's hulking form waited on the other side. Bradley. Of course it was Bradley.

He pushed inside and closed the door, latching each of the locks. His hands remained steady, calm, without a hint of anxiety. He strode across the room and put his gun on the table with a thud. When he turned to Julianne, genuine concern stained his eyes. "Are you okay?"

Julianne nodded, even though she didn't feel that way. She hadn't felt okay in a while, and she had doubts she'd feel okay in the future even. "Did you see anyone?"

"No, he got away. He jumped on a motorcycle and fled before I could catch him."

The blood drained from her face. "Darrell rode a motorcycle." Her words sounded raw, just above a whisper, and each syllable tight with strain.

Bradley nodded, the lines constricting on his face. "I know."

She rubbed her cheek and closed her eyes. This had to be a nightmare. Would it ever end? "Do you believe me now?" She didn't bother to open her eyes and see his expression.

"I never said I didn't believe you."

She opened her eyes—just slightly, enough that they were narrow with suspicion. "You never said you did, either."

He stared at her a moment, saying nothing until he finally mumbled, "I should be going. I'm going to set the alarm. It will go off if anyone tries to get in."

"Good to know."

"Good night, Julianne."

Against her better judgment, she smiled. "Good night, Bradley."

The next morning, Bradley felt as if he'd battled a hurricane. He hadn't been able to get back to sleep after he'd spotted the man lurking outside the house. Instead, he'd remained on guard, pacing from window to window for a sign that the intruder had returned.

He'd seen nothing.

He had, however, downed two pots of coffee, and now a strange mixture of exhaustion and caffeine mingled in his blood, promising him that the day would be long. He set his mug on the kitchen counter and started down the hallway just as the sun began to rise over the ocean.

He had to get showered and dressed for work.

And he had to figure out what to do with Julianne. He couldn't exactly leave her here all day by herself. She had no car or money. She'd be practically helpless—other than the lamp stand that she'd brandished last night.

He smiled at the memory. Though he didn't want to admit it—to himself, even—she'd looked adorable with her hair tussled, wearing an oversize T-shirt and exercise pants, and holding that oversize lamp left over by the previous owner.

His smile slipped when he also remembered her fear. No, he couldn't leave her here alone all day. Which meant he'd have to bring her with him to work. But what would he do with her there?

He'd figure it out, one way or another.

A few minutes later, he trudged down the steps with two cups of coffee in hand. He set the drinks on a patio table located on the driveway beneath the home, and then knocked on the door. When Julianne opened the door, he blinked at the sight of her.

Elle had brought her some clothes that seemed to fit her perfectly. She wore no make-up, but she didn't need any. The woman's skin was flawless. Even her hair looked great with a slight touch of wave in the still-damp tresses.

He grabbed the coffee and handed her one as he stepped inside. He caught a whiff of soap, the scent fresh and clean, as he breezed past.

Just because he was attracted to the woman did

not mean he had to act on any of those feelings. Beautiful women were a dime a dozen, and he had other more important issues to think about—issues like national security.

He cleared his throat. Despite his reasoning, Julianne was still enough to take his breath away. Which brought him to ask his next question. "How'd you sleep?" That was a safe subject, though he could probably guess her answer.

She shrugged and took a sip of coffee before answering. "I didn't. Every little squeak I heard had me on edge."

He gripped his coffee, suddenly feeling the need to retreat from the cozy space he shared with Julianne. She was too close and caused his heart to twist with desire...and with loss and grief and anger. He took a step back. "I was wondering how you felt about going with me to work today. I'd feel better if you weren't alone."

She blinked as if his words surprised her. "I appreciate the gesture. I promise I'll be quiet and stay out of your way."

Guilt trickled through him. There was a good chance this woman didn't like the circumstance she'd been thrust into the middle of any more than he did. He had to give her the benefit of the doubt, no matter how crazy her story sounded. He could give her a chance, he reminded himself, while still keeping her at arms' distance.

He nodded toward the door. "Let's get on the road, then. I have a full day."

She paused for a moment, standing close enough to him that he could see the flecks of blue in her hazel eyes. Something about her gaze made him want to stare into those eyes all day. "I mean it when I said I really appreciate this."

He stepped back, not liking the way his heart sped at her closeness. "I'm glad I can help." But was he? Was he glad? Not really. He had little choice but to help. He wouldn't tell her that, though.

He opened the door to the SUV for her, waited for Julianne to climb inside and then hurried to the driver's side. Why did riding to work with her—and having his heart race the way it did—make him feel like he was betraying his late fiancée? he wondered. As he started down the road, Vanessa's memory caused loss to burn in his gut. She'd been one of the few people he'd allowed inside his walls, one of the few women to make his heart pound without logic. She'd been sweet, knowing exactly how to coax him out of a bad mood, knowing just how to make his day brighter with her laughter and smile.

They'd met through a mutual friend, and he'd instantly noticed a kindness about her. He'd spontaneously asked her if she'd like to go out sometime. She'd smiled, her eyes twinkling, and said yes. They were inseparable after that. Six months later, they were engaged. Six months after that, she'd been killed. He hadn't been the same man since then. He'd always been quiet and to himself, but those qualities became even more prevalent after her death.

He mourned and fought anger over the senseless taking of a life. Those emotions had seemed to choke him, sucking him into a reclusive little world. Not even his friends at Eyes had been able to break down his walls, though they tried. He still did his job—maybe with even more drive and excellence than before. He poured himself into his work to try to ward away the emotions that seemed so foreign to him.

After all, he was a soldier. He fought for what he believed in. He stood up for the men under him. He was diligent and trustworthy and hardworking. But feeling vengeance and heart-wrenching grief…those weren't things he had to deal with, weren't things that he'd been equipped to face. No one could prepare him to lose his soul mate.

"Do you think we should report the last night's intruder to the police?" Julianne's voice pulled him from his thoughts.

Vanessa's picture disappeared from his mind. He already missed the warmth her memory had brought. "Probably won't do any good. There's no evidence. Just our word—my word, I suppose, since you didn't see him."

She nodded, that same heaviness seeming to return to her. What wasn't this woman telling him? Her gaze focused out the window.

He cleared his throat again. "Tell me about your relationship with Darrell, Julianne."

She swallowed and licked her lips. "What about it?"

"How'd you meet?"

She rubbed her hands against her jeans. "We met at a concert down at the beach. He was there with some friends. I'm pretty sure one of them dared him to come talk to me and, of course, he did. Told me he was a SEAL. I didn't believe him, but he did charm me enough that I gave him my phone number. I didn't think he'd actually call."

"But he did." That sounded like the Darrell that Bradley knew.

She sighed. "He did. We met for ice cream on the boardwalk. He told me that it was love at first sight and that he was going to marry me."

"How'd you react to that?"

She shrugged, a sad smile curling the side of her lip. "I guess I was flattered. I mean, he was a good-looking guy. He had charisma and guts and a smile that knocked my socks off."

"Come on, you're no ugly duckling. I'm sure men have used a lot of lines on you over the years."

She glanced at him, her eyes widening in surprise. Maybe he shouldn't have admitted that she was beautiful, even if he'd said it in the most factual way possible. "I'd just broken up with a boyfriend of two years after I'd found out he was cheating on me. I was feeling pretty low and vulnerable. Darrell told me just what I wanted to hear, I suppose. It felt good to know that someone thought I was desirable."

He didn't know what to say. Guys stood in line to date a girl like Julianne. But past relationships could affect the psyche so deeply. The thought of men treating someone with such a sweet spirit so poorly made anger warm his blood.

"You know, I was always the type of girl who had a boyfriend, ever since I was a teenager. I didn't know what it was like to be single." She cleared her throat. "But my life's totally different now. I like being single, for the most part, at least. It's made me realize that I can't find happiness in any man."

"Wise words."

"It wasn't the easiest lesson to learn, but God brings us to the places we're supposed to be. I guess I need to remember that now."

It was a good reminder for him, too. He believed in God's plan and purpose in his life, but he didn't talk about God like Julianne did, with such a personal feel. Maybe he needed to start doing that.

He glanced over at her. "As soon as this is over,

you'll have your full independence back. Until then, I think it's best if you lay low."

"I don't have much choice, do I?"

"You always have choices." He slowed at a turn in the road. "If you think it would be better, I'd be happy to loan you some money so you can get out of here." Now why had he offered that? And why did he hold his breath in fear that she might actually say yes?

"You would do that for me?"

He shrugged. "I don't want you to feel like you're being held against your will due to unforeseen circumstances. I could give you money to get a car and make it for a month or so until you get on your feet again."

"That's really generous of you, Bradley. Thank you, but I think I will stay put. I don't know where else I'd go." She sighed. "My best friend just moved to California, so I suppose I could go there, but I just feel like Darrell would find me there, too. That he'll always find me."

He wondered about her choice of words. The wistfulness by which she said them made Bradley think she'd felt like that for a long time now. Or was he reading too much into this?

They stopped in front of Eyes headquarters, passing the guard station and parking in front of the main building. If only he knew he could trust Julianne, it would make his day so much easier. But doubts still nagged at the back of his mind. What wasn't Julianne telling him?

They walked upstairs to his office, calling out hellos to a few people as they passed. He paused at the desk outside his workspace. Diane, his secretary, wasn't here…again. Where was the woman? Would he have another voicemail from her with some kind of excuse? The next time he saw her, they would sit down and have a serious talk about responsibility.

He paused and glanced over at Julianne. She stood there, looking at him with wide, doelike eyes that made him feel guilty for ever doubting her innocence. "Why don't you have a seat and make yourself comfortable out here while I work? There are some magazines and books." He pointed to two wingback chairs in the corner with a table crammed full of reading literature between them.

She nodded stiffly. "I'll be fine. I need to call work and check in, anyway."

He hesitated before going into his office and leaving the door open. To keep an eye on her for fear she'd do something she shouldn't…or out of concern for her well-being? He wasn't sure.

He sat at his desk and attempted to focus on the tasks at hand. He was only thirty minutes into his work when his phone rang. It was one of the guards stationed by the gate. What now?

"There are two police detectives at the gate. They need to talk to you."

Bradley tensed. "Did they say about what?"

"About your secretary, sir."

SIX

The serious undertones of Bradley's voice pricked Julianne's curiosity, as well as incited the all-too-familiar feeling of dread in her stomach. What was the phone call about? A moment later, Bradley stepped back into the reception area, and Julianne looked up from the seat where she'd been checking her emails on her phone.

The man always looked serious, but right now the hardness of his face seemed even more impenetrable. She had the crazy urge to go over to him and touch his cheek, to tell him that everything would be all right…which was ironic when considering that she herself didn't feel as if everything would be all right.

Bradley stood in the doorway and swallowed hard enough that Julianne could sense his tension. "My secretary, Diane…she's missing. Her son reported it to the police this morning. They're here to ask a few questions."

Julianne's heart lurched. Another person in danger? Could this be connected with Darrell? That didn't even sound reasonable.

She shivered and pulled her arms over her chest. All of these things happening at one time couldn't be a coincidence. It just couldn't.

Bradley's gaze locked on hers. "Why don't you join me? I'm meeting them downstairs."

The tone of his voice held an edge to it. He couldn't very well leave her in his office alone. She was sure there were probably top-secret files here and that she'd need some kind of clearance. So it appeared that Bradley was stuck with her.

They walked in silence downstairs where they saw Detective Spencer again, along with another suited man. Bradley greeted them both with a handshake and then nodded down the corridor. "How about we go into the conference room?"

The detectives agreed. A moment later, they were situated in a plain room with a large table and a dozen chairs. Bradley looked like his normal, at ease, professional self while Julianne wanted to crawl into a corner and hide.

Why did she feel guilty, as if this were her fault? She didn't know his secretary. She didn't even know what had happened yet. Still, sorrow pounded through her veins. She distanced herself from the rest of the people at the table, putting a chair between them and herself. Bradley glanced over at her, his gaze ever perceptive.

Did he hold her responsible for this?

"Mr. Stone, when was the last time you spoke to Mrs. Hewitt?"

"She didn't come into work yesterday, but she's had a lot of family issues going on lately, so I didn't think much of it. It hasn't been unusual for her to come in late or to leave early, or for her to make several personal phone calls during the day. I tried to give her some leeway since I knew she was going through a hard divorce."

So the man *did* have a softer side. Maybe what Elle had told Julianne was true. Could Bradley really be one of the kindest people she'd ever meet? Was his compassion hidden behind his tough alpha-male exterior? She wasn't convinced yet.

"Was the divorce ugly? Any signs that her estranged husband is capable of violence?"

Julianne gasped at the question. Men capable of violence against women… It was such a crime. A tragedy. A heartbreaking reality of which she was all too aware.

Bradley glanced at her again before looking back at the detective. "None that I know of. Every divorce is ugly but their kids are grown. As divorces go, it seemed pretty civil."

"Is there anyone you can think of who'd want to hurt Diane?"

Bradley shifted. "No, not directly. However, I do know that the technology I'm developing is sought after by groups other than the Defense Department—groups who'd pay a hefty fee to get it into their own hands."

"You mean terrorist organizations?"

Julianne listened in fascination. Just what was Bradley developing? She'd heard him talking about some urgent projects, but she had no idea of the exact scope of his work. A touch of pride and awe welled in her. The man may lack people skills, but he had a heart for keeping soldiers safe. Who wouldn't admire that?

Bradley laced his fingers together on the table. "That's correct. Perhaps someone thought if they could get to Diane, they could get to us also."

Which might explain some of Bradley's suspicions concerning her appearance here. In his line of work, he had to be cautious. The information and technology he was developing would certainly be a hot commodity in the hands of the enemy.

Detective Spencer and his partner stood. The lead detective offered a crisp nod. "I'd suggest keeping an eye on everyone surrounding this project, Mr. Stone. You're a security contractor, so I'm sure you realize the risks."

"We've been on heightened alert, and we'll remain that way." Bradley's face tightened a moment as he rose to his feet also. "If you don't mind me asking, were there any signs of struggle? Is there anything else you can tell me about Diane's disappearance?"

Detective Spencer's expression remained grim. "I can tell you that the last time she was seen was two days ago. A neighbor saw her come home from the grocery store. No one's heard from her since then. Her car is in the driveway, but the groceries were still on the kitchen counter, never put away. There was no sign of struggle."

Bradley nodded, still solemn as they all walked toward the door and into the lobby area. "What can we do?"

"Nothing. Just keep your eyes and ears open. If you hear anything, let us know." The detective paused. "Could we take a look at her desk? See if there's anything there that might give us a clue as to what happened?"

"Absolutely."

As they walked up the steps, Julianne caught up to Detective Spencer. She rubbed her sweaty hands on her jeans as her nerves got the best of her. "Excuse me, detective. If you don't mind me asking, how's the mechanic?"

"He's doing better. I think he'll recover from this just fine."

Relief filled her. But only for a moment. She quickened her steps to keep up. "Any updates on what happened?"

"The ignition was rigged. It could have easily been you in the hospital. Or worse—the morgue."

They reached the second level and started toward Bradley's office. "Were you able to get any evidence? Anything that might tell you who did this?" She was probably asking too many questions, but she couldn't stop herself.

He paused and glanced at her, his eyes kind but weary. "We're working on it. But nothing yet. Give us some time. I assure you, we're doing our best to get to the bottom of this."

Julianne nodded and crossed her arms over her chest. She remained in the hallway as the detectives checked Diane's desk. They left several moments later.

When they were out of earshot, Bradley turned to her. His hands went to his hips. That, coupled with the sports jacket and tie he wore, made him seem even more dynamic than usual. The man exuded strength and bravado. "Julianne, I have to ask you a question."

Dread pooled in her stomach, but she managed a nod. "Okay."

His gaze fixed on hers with a look that would unnerve the most dangerous of criminals. "Do you know anything about Diane's disappearance?"

His words—and their implications—slammed into her heart. She blinked, feeling as if she'd been physically hit. Then she raised her chin. "What are you suggesting?"

"I'm just asking a question." His voice sounded softer, but she didn't care. What would she have to do to prove her innocence? To prove that she was a victim here?

Julianne shook her head, fire running through her veins. She'd vowed that she'd never let herself feel small at the hands of a man again. Never. Bradley Stone was no exception. "What kind of fool do you take me for? There are serious implications behind that inquiry, Mr. Stone. And to answer your question…no, I don't know anything. I don't know Diane. I didn't know she was going to disappear. I didn't know any of this was going to happen."

He stepped back, his gaze hot on hers. "I see."

Her hand went to her hip. "You *see?* You really think I had something to do with all of this?" Her voice rose in pitch with each word.

"I have to explore every possibility."

"Then explore the possibility that maybe you're the link here. Maybe she was abducted because of her work for you." She turned on her heel. "Now, if you'll excuse me…I need to call my coworkers and tell them why I'm a no-show today."

Bradley watched Julianne go. He regretted his words, but he'd felt as if he had to ask. None of this craziness started until Julianne showed up. Sure, there had been some threats and some intercepted communications that indicated his work was a hot commodity on the black market. But nothing had ever come of it.

Even more prevalent than his worry over offending Julianne, there was his worry over Diane's safety. The woman had only worked here a few months, not long enough for Bradley to get to know her really. She'd always seemed nice enough and, until the past couple of weeks, she'd seemed efficient. She was fifty-one with two grown boys—one was in college locally and the other had just taken a job up in D.C.

D.C.

That's where Julianne lived. Was that the connection? He didn't know. He couldn't put his finger on it yet; he just knew that something wasn't adding up. He needed to figure out what. Diane couldn't possibly be in on all of this, could she? No, Julianne had brought trouble with her. He'd hired Diane long before Julianne showed up here.

As he went into his office, Julianne didn't look up from her phone. She was upset, and rightfully so. She was going to have to face him again, though. She didn't have much of a choice, especially not when her life and the lives of others were on the line.

He sat at Diane's desk and glanced around. Were there any clues here as to her disappearance? He glanced at her calendar. Nothing out of the ordinary caught his eye. He opened a drawer, flipped through some papers looking for something—anything—that might offer a clue.

A phone number had been scribbled on a piece of paper. Why did the number look familiar?

"Julianne, can I see your phone?"

She glanced up sharply, and although he half expected her to refuse, she shrugged instead. "Go for it. I have nothing to hide." She strode across the room and handed it to him—more like smacked it into his hand. She stood there and crossed her arms over her chest.

He looked at her call history.

There. There it was.

Darrell Lewis's phone number was the one that had been stashed in Diane's desk drawer.

So Diane and Darrell had been in contact?

And now Julianne had shown up here? He looked up at her, at the scowl on her face as she glowered down at him.

None of the puzzle pieces were fitting together. He'd thought it was because they were all from different puzzles.

But what if they weren't?

What if somehow they were all connected?

"I have no idea why she would have the number. No idea." Julianne wrapped her arms around herself. Could get this get any worse? She had a feeling she didn't want to know the answer. Things were escalating, and now a woman was missing.

Had Darrell grabbed her? Why? And, if so, what had he done with her?

Nothing made sense.

Her life felt as if it was spiraling out of control and there was nothing she could do about it. Alan was dead. John was dead. Diane was MIA. Bradley, the one person who could help her, suspected she was somehow involved.

But there something else that didn't compute—something major. If Diane had disappeared two days ago, that was before Julianne showed up here. She'd assumed Darrell was only targeting people that she'd been in contact with.

But what if Darrell had targeted Diane also? Why would he do that? What was she overlooking here?

The desk phone rang. Bradley stared at it a moment but made no move to answer.

Julianne pointed to the phone. "You're not going to get that?"

"I don't have time to monitor my calls. I'm already behind." He sighed, and Julianne noticed the exhaustion around his eyes.

Because of her. He didn't say that, but he probably wanted to.

"How about if I make myself useful and answer the phone for you?"

He leaned back as if contemplating his response.

Meanwhile, the phone continued to jangle. "Do you have any experience?"

"I answer phones for a living. Of course, it's a hotline…but still. I like to think I have some skills in that department." She stared at him, daring him to look away.

She'd been placed in a situation where she had no choice but to ask for help, but that didn't mean she wasn't capable. She prided herself on being organized, efficient and compassionately discerning. Discernment came in handy when she counseled people.

She took each of her clients seriously, but there had been a few occasions where callers had been little more than pranksters. Then there was that one caller who'd given her the creeps. He'd kept calling and asking for her, asking her personal questions. He'd even come down to their office once and tried to find her. Thank goodness he hadn't seen her.

Of course, she hadn't seen him, either. Could it have been…Darrell?

She shook off those thoughts as Bradley stood. "I'd appreciate it then. I need to lock myself in the office for the rest of the day, so if you could just take messages for me."

Julianne plopped into the seat, a moment of guilt filling her as she realized that Diane should be here. *God, please watch over her. Help her to be okay. Keep her from harm.*

Bradley gave her a lingering glance before going into his office. Once again, he didn't shut the door—probably because he wanted to keep tabs on her, which was fine by Julianne. He'd see that she was trustworthy.

The rest of the day passed uneventfully. The detective came back and got the scrap of paper, and Julianne answered several phone calls, taking messages just as Bradley had directed.

Close to five o'clock, her cell phone rang. Her work cell phone. She'd been on call since she left, but this was the first hotline call she'd received. At least, she assumed it was a hotline call since she didn't recognize the number.

"This is Julianne. I'm here to remind you that there's always hope. What can I do for you today?"

Silence stretched on the other line.

"Hello?" she repeated. Still, she heard no one, only a faint crackle that caused her nerves to rev. She wanted to hang up. But what if it was someone who needed her help? Who was simply afraid to begin speaking? She couldn't hang up based on some irrational fear.

"I'm here if you need to talk and tell me what's going on in your life."

"Julianne." The word was whispered, so soft that she thought she'd imagined it. Had she?

Suddenly, she couldn't say anything, do anything. The phone felt frozen to ear.

"It's all for you." The same whisper, one that sent chills all over her skin.

A shadow passed in the distance. Bradley. Standing in the doorway, his hands on his hips, worry wrinkling between his eyes.

She bristled, realizing she had to seize this opportunity. This was her chance to get some answers. "What's all for me? What are you talking about? Who is this?"

Silence stretched out for several long seconds. The phone line cackled and cracked. Someone was on the other line. He just wasn't speaking. Her gut tightened. That's when she heard the breathing—deep, raspy breaths. Breaths that were meant to be known, breaths that were purposeful.

"What's all for me?"

More silence and breathing and crackling. Normally, she might try to prod a little more, to coax the person on the other line into talking. But the events of the past twenty-four hours were playing mind tricks on her, making her suspicious of everything and everyone.

She pulled the phone from her ear, ready to hang up when she heard someone speak on the other end.

"I need help." The voice was gravelly and low.

"Why don't you tell me what's going on?" Was this Darrell or was she reading too much into things? She had to keep a level head.

"All I can think about is death."

Shivers raced up her spine. "Death? Why do you suppose that is? Did something happen?"

"I'm angry. People have said I'm possessive. And I have no hope so I have nothing to lose."

Her shivers intensified. She'd gotten some weird calls before—calls where the absence of emotion in people's voices made her blood turn cold. This man might outweigh the rest of those calls, though. His voice, his words… She didn't like where this was going.

"There's always hope for whatever you're facing. There's always help available. Calling this hotline was a good first step."

"Are you sure?"

"Of course. I want to help you and I want you to know that taking your life is never the answer."

"I never said I was considering taking my own life, Julianne. I'm thinking about taking other people's. Starting with Bradley Stone."

Julianne gasped. Darrell. She was talking to Darrell.

And he wanted to kill Bradley.

SEVEN

Bradley saw Julianne's face go stark white—again. But as her eyes met his across the room, fear and sorrow loomed in their depths. Just who was on the other end of that phone call?

She pulled the phone from her ear. "He's gone. He hung up."

"Who's gone?"

"Darrell." Her voice hitched as she said the word.

Bradley straightened. "That was Darrell? Darrell actually called you?"

"He didn't say his name, but it was him. I know it was." She pulled her arms over her chest and stared at the cell phone laying on the desk in front of her.

"What did he say?" He stepped closer, protectiveness rising in him.

When she looked up at him, the fear in her eyes was truly palpable. "He said he's going to kill you."

Bradley leaned against the desk, certain he hadn't understood her correctly. "Darrell said he was going to kill me? He used my name?"

She nodded.

"Why would he want to kill me?" This situation was becoming more absurd by the moment.

She shook her head, her fearful expression morphing into outrage. "Why would he do anything that he's done? Nothing makes sense. He doesn't make sense."

"Why do you think he would fake his death, Julianne? What reason would he have for doing that?" He kept his voice even, trying to dispel any panic and keep Julianne calm.

"I've thought about that a thousand times. I don't know. He wanted out of the military? He wanted to escape his life? Maybe more sinister reasons. Maybe he started working for an enemy of the United States and he needed to die before he was found out. I really have no idea."

"Why would he want to kill the people around you? Why chance coming out of hiding to risk that, especially if he was successful in faking his death?" He needed a plausible explanation and so far he didn't have one.

She rubbed her shoulder. She did that a lot when she was nervous or scared, he noted.

"He told me once that if he couldn't have me, no one could. I think he might be targeting anyone he sees as a threat." She stood so quickly that her chair rammed into a trashcan and sent it toppling over. "I should go. I should take you up on that offer to loan me some money and get out of here. I can't stand the thought of causing someone else's death."

"Julianne—"

Desperate eyes met his. She stepped closer, her gaze pleading. "So what do you say? Can I still borrow the money?"

He inhaled deeply. She was like a frightened rabbit, ready to run. However, she wasn't thinking about herself. She was frightened for others, wanting to protect those around her. He couldn't let her do that, though he admired the noble thought. It made him want to protect her even more. "I can take care of myself, Julianne. Don't worry about me."

"You don't know what he's capable of." Her voice went eerily still.

"I have a good idea."

Her intense gaze met his. "You have no idea." Her voice was barely above a whisper.

He stepped closer. "Why don't you tell me?"

At once, she scooted back and shook her head, almost as if some kind of instinct kicked in. She squeezed her eyes closed and drew in several deep breaths. "Just answer my question. Can I still borrow that money and get out of town?"

"No." He said it in a way that left no room for argument.

She blinked. "No? But just this morning..."

Against his better judgment, he laid his hand on

Julianne's arm. He felt her tense and wanted more than anything to comfort her. "I don't think you're in any state of mind to strike out on your own. I'd feel better if I could keep an eye on you."

"You don't have to do that," she rasped. She rubbed her shoulder again, almost with a certain fury.

"I don't have to do a lot of things, Julianne. I *want* to."

"But your life could be in danger." Her voice cracked with emotion.

"Like I said, I can take care of myself. Don't worry about me. I've faced some pretty formidable enemies before. I didn't come out untouched, but I came out stronger."

Her arm trembled under his touch, and her eyes glimmered with unshed tears.

He directed her back to the seat in the corner and lowered her there. "Why don't you sit down for a moment? I have a few things I need to wrap up. You're safe here. As soon as I'm done, we'll go back to the house. It's going to be okay. You hear me?"

She nodded, but her eyes didn't register the assurance.

"Why don't you turn that phone off? If Darrell is trying to scare you, it's working. No need to give him any more power." He'd play along. He'd pretend that Darrell really was alive, even if he had his doubts. Either way, he had to get to the bottom of this.

Something was obviously going on. Though he knew he should probably assign someone else to watch over Julianne, he couldn't bring himself to do it. He needed to know for himself that she was safe and taken care of. Maybe he could protect her, even if he hadn't been able to protect Vanessa.

Vanessa.

Every time he thought of her, his heart throbbed with sadness. Last week would have been their wedding. He'd wanted to get married sooner. She'd insisted on waiting, said she needed more time to plan her dream wedding. He'd wanted to give her everything and anything she'd wanted so, of course, he'd complied. Now he wished he'd insisted on pushing up the wedding. Maybe things would have been different.

"Bradley?" Julianne blinked at him, and he realized he was staring at her.

He stood. "You're going to be okay. I'll make sure of it."

Julianne stared out the car window at the darkness around them. The car was silent—no radio, no chatter, no GPS telling them where to go. All she heard was the turn of tires on pavement and the sound of other cars zooming past.

The harder she thought about everything, the

more her head hurt. She wished the end was in sight, but she realized that even when she found some answers, her life would still be in danger. How would she pick up all the pieces and reach a semblance of normalcy again?

She pushed the thought aside and turned toward Bradley. They drove off the main road, going in the opposite direction from his house. "Where are we going?"

"I thought you might want to grab a bite to eat before going back to my place."

She was hungry, now that he mentioned it. She'd grabbed a sandwich down in the cafeteria for lunch, but that had been five or six hours ago now. "Sounds good."

"Like seafood?"

"I do." Not that it was usually her cuisine of choice, but she wasn't going to argue. How could she? She was reliant on Bradley for everything right now...a fact that she wasn't entirely comfortable with. She liked being independent. But was that even an option now? She knew the answer—no. But she'd put this behind her and, when she did, she'd make a way for herself again. With God's help, of course.

They drove down to the resort area of Virginia Beach, a picturesque place with tall hotels, gift shops and restaurants along the boardwalk. In the summer, this part of town was flooded with tourists. But in the winter, the streets were mostly barren.

Bradley pulled into the Rudee Inlet, an area a few blocks away from the boardwalk, and stopped in front of a seafood restaurant. The waterway was popular with boaters, fishermen and tourist expeditions like parasailing and dolphin-watching tours.

They walked toward an octagon-shaped, plank-sided building, up a flight of stairs and stepped into the dining area. The place was filled with mounted replicas of fish, carved wooden fishermen and old fishing nets decorated with sand dollars, sea stars and shells. Despite the simple decor, the price per plate deemed it upscale. Julianne knew because she'd eaten here once before. They were seated at a window table facing the inlet. In the darkness outside, water glimmered under a few stray streetlights. A couple of guys—fishermen, she assumed—walked along a nearby dock.

"I'm from Texas, you know." Bradley followed her gaze. "I came here when I was a SEAL and fell in love with the area. Never wanted to go back."

"It is nice being so close to the ocean."

"How about you? Where are you from?"

"I was born out in the western part of the state, in Roanoke, to be exact. Came here to get a job after college, and ended up staying. Until Darrell died, at least. Then I moved up north to the D.C. area."

"Why'd you move?"

His question caught her by surprise, and she shrugged, trying to buy time as a waitress set a basket of cornbread on the table along with two glasses of water. She picked up her glass and twirled the ice around with her straw before looking up at him. "I just needed a change, I suppose."

Bradley stared at her a moment longer. He obviously knew there was something she wasn't telling him. But how could she tell him the truth? She'd only appear weak. He'd only pity her. She wanted neither of those things. She had to keep some of her pride intact, didn't she? She had no one else to protect her. She only had herself and God to rely on.

She distracted herself by perusing the menu. A few minutes later, she ordered soup and Bradley ordered some broiled salmon. With their menus gone, silence stretched between them. Darkness, which had begun to fall when they left the Eyes headquarters, now stained the sky an inky black. Lights reflected onto the dark water outside their window. This was the perfect spot for a romantic dinner for two. If only this were a romantic dinner instead of an obligatory gathering of two people with nothing in common except a lunatic.

"Will you go with me for a moment on something?" Bradley stared at her from across the table.

"I suppose." She picked up some corn bread and slathered some butter across it.

"Let's assume for a moment that Darrell isn't behind any of this. Are there any other possibilities?"

Julianne bit down on her lip. Darrell was at the center of this, but she could be levelheaded enough to explore other options. "It would have to be someone who knew about Darrell, who knew how he acted and what he liked."

"A friend maybe?"

She shrugged and then her eyes lit with a memory. "I did run into Tommy Sanders about a month ago."

Bradley straightened, his expression filling with curiosity. "Tommy Sanders? There's a name I haven't heard in a long time."

She leaned back in her chair, her stomach rumbling with hunger. "It was the strangest thing. I went down to see my parents here in Virginia Beach before they left for their cruise. We went out to dinner out in Lynnhaven, and he was there at the restaurant having dinner with a friend."

"Did he act strangely?"

"Now that you mention it, he did. He seemed uncomfortable…and he had shifty eyes. I just thought it was because of Darrell, like he didn't know how to express his grief still or something."

"That was the first time you'd seen him since…?"

"Since Darrell's funeral." She nodded. "Yeah, I didn't really stick around the military community afterward. I lost touch with almost everyone."

"Anyone else who's given you the creeps? Left you with an unsettled feeling?"

Julianne shook her head. "No, not really. I mean, I guess there was that one guy who always called the hotline and asked for me."

"Tell me about him."

She told Bradley about how the caller always asked personal questions and seemed to know more about her than he should. But she'd never seen the man, and he hadn't reached out in a couple of weeks. Of course, she had no name or face for the man, either.

The waitress set their food on the table, giving them a reprieve from the heavy conversation. They ate in comfortable silence for a few minutes. The crab soup tasted creamy and spicy and warm—the perfect meal for the cold day.

Julianne glanced out the window a moment and watched a few people on the docks below. She straightened when she thought she saw a familiar face watching from the shadows. Oval face, light brown hair, buzz cut.

No. It couldn't be. Or was it?

"Julianne?"

She pointed outside. "I thought I saw…" She couldn't complete the sentence. Was her mind playing tricks on her?

"Saw what?"

She drew a deep breath. "Darrell."

He stood, his gaze firm as it met hers. "Stay here. Understand?"

She'd only begun to nod when Bradley raced out of the room. She sat at the table, her fingers nervously rubbing the napkin in her lap. She couldn't sit still any longer. She began pacing, ignoring the strange looks from the wait staff and the other patrons.

She paused and pressed her face against the glass. A figure darted from the shadows—from the same area where Julianne had thought she'd seen Darrell. A moment later, Bradley appeared with gun in hand.

Where did Darrell go? Where had he disappeared to this time? The man was like a shadow that disappeared with the wind.

Movement to the left caught her eye. Somehow, the man was behind Bradley now. Her heart leaped into her throat. What if he shot Bradley? What if he made good on his threat?

She couldn't wait any longer. She ran out the door and around the deck that stretched the length of the restaurant. She leaned over the railing, desperate to get Bradley's attention. "Bradley, watch out!"

Just as she shouted the words, a shot rang out. She ducked down toward the railing, a flimsy shield of protection but all she had at the moment. Slowly, she stood, keeping one eye open for a sign of what had just happened. She saw no one. Who had fired that gun?

Someone gripped her from behind, his fingers like a metal clamp. The man jerked her back. "Don't turn around. You're coming with me."

She froze. The voice wasn't Darrell's. He didn't smell like Darrell and the projection of his voice made her think he was at least four inches shorter.

Something sharp pressed into her side.

She shuddered, wondering if this would be her last breath. "You've got the wrong person."

"I know exactly who you are, señorita. Now move."

"I don't know anything." She had to stall for time. Things wouldn't end this way. She wouldn't let it.

"I'll be the judge of that." The man had an accent. A Mexican accent? It was her best guess. "Move."

"I'm not going anywhere." She wouldn't come back alive if she did—she was sure of it. In a desperate attempt to stay put, she dug her heels into the wooden planks of the deck. Its rough edges and frequent gaps offered natural resistance.

"Julianne!" At the sound of Bradley's voice, she threw herself to the ground. Something sharp sliced into her, sending pain ripping through her shoulder. Still, she clawed away from the man, fighting for her life.

A gun fired, and the man behind her moaned. Then she heard footsteps. He was getting away, leaving a trail of blood. Could she stop him? She grasped her shoulder. No, she'd never get to him in time.

Another gunshot pierced the air.

Someone screamed in the distance. Another person shouted. More footsteps pounded.

She didn't dare stand. Not when she knew a bullet could still reach her. Her head swam, and panic seemed to charge through her bloodstream.

Bradley. Was he okay? Had the shooter gotten to him?

A moment later, two hands grasped her arms. "Julianne, you're bleeding."

She looked up, blinking until Bradley came into focus. Bradley. He was okay. Thank goodness he was okay. "Did you get Darrell?"

His face, all serious and tight with worry, was inches from hers as he inspected her. "No, he got away. So did the man who grabbed you. Any idea who he was?"

She shook her head, trying to ignore the throbbing pain in her shoulder. "I've never seen him before."

Bradley helped her to her feet, surprisingly gentle. "Come on. We've got to get out of here before someone else tries to get to you."

"But the police? Shouldn't we call the police?"

"I'll call them en route. Right now, you're an open target…and I don't like it."

The cut across Julianne's shoulder burned. The knife had gone deep enough that she felt woozy. Bradley wanted to take her to the hospital, but she'd refused. What she really wanted was to go somewhere safe, and right now Bradley's home felt safe to her.

Bradley cut the engine as they pulled to a stop in front of his beach house. With one arm around her waist and his solid muscles holding her upright, he helped her up the stairs, one by one. The winter wind, frigid from the ocean, swept around them and added to her misery.

Finally, they stepped inside his house. The cold from outside was warded away by the heavy steel door and top-grade windows. Never had a place seemed so welcoming.

Bradley led her to his couch and lowered her there. "I need to see your shoulder."

The blood drained from her face. Her shoulder… her injured shoulder. He'd see the ugly, scarred skin. He'd be repulsed. *She* was repulsed.

She started to shake her head no, but she had to get the wound examined. She didn't want to risk infection. She couldn't afford the doctor, and she wouldn't take any more of Bradley's charity.

So what if he sees your scar? So what if he's

repulsed? It wasn't like Julianne had hopes of a future with him.

Bradley knelt in front of her. His gaze locked on hers. The expression on his face conveyed that he'd seen his fair share of battle scars before. Clearly, this was a man who'd been thrust into unimaginable circumstances and knew how to handle himself. His strength seemed to transfer to her through his touch. She needed that right now.

"We need to get some antibiotic on it, Julianne."

She bit her lip, trying to ignore the tears that popped into her eyes as she gripped the edge of her sweatshirt. Thankfully, she wore a tank top underneath. Slowly, uncertainly, and through the stinging pain, she tugged the sweatshirt off.

She held her breath as she waited to see his expression, waited to see his face when he saw the grotesque scar.

His eyes widened. His fingers went to the pink flesh at her neck, and his thumb rubbed a mark there. His touch was so tender, his gaze so full of concern.

"Julianne..."

She didn't dare look him in the eye.

His hand slid down her arm until he gripped her fingers. She could feel his blistering gaze on her, begging her to look at him. She couldn't. "What happened?"

She shrugged. "Long story."

"I have time."

"I don't want to talk about it." She just wanted to get her wound treated, put her sweatshirt back on and retreat by herself. She couldn't bear Bradley's pity. Did he enjoy her humiliation? No, she knew he didn't. He wasn't that type of man. She'd felt so self-conscious about her scar for so long.

Darrell's plan had worked. He'd made her feel unattractive. He'd won, she realized, more tears welling in her eyes.

"Let me get you bandaged up." Gently, he cleaned her wound before putting some gauze and medical tape around it.

They said nothing, but the tension stretched between them said enough. Julianne was aware of his every movement, his every touch, his every breath for that matter.

"All done," he finally said. He rubbed the last of the medical tape down, letting his fingers trail her arm in the process.

She cleared her throat and rushed to her feet, unsure of what to do with the mixed feelings waging a war inside her. Humiliation, shame, disappointment—in herself mostly—and a deep, undeniable attraction to Bradley Stone. She hadn't even realized the attraction was there until this moment.

She pushed a hair behind her ear. "Thank you. I should go."

Bradley stood also, and she was painfully cognizant of his every movement. "Julianne."

She paused. She shouldn't have. She should have run. Instead, she made eye contact with Bradley. Before she realized what was happening, he stepped toward her.

His fingers fanned out on her neck and into her hair. Then his lips were on hers. Tender, passionate, causing her to gravitate toward him, propelling her hand to grip his shirt. Her lips tingled. Her heart raced. And her mind was swirling with reasons why this shouldn't be happening.

Bradley's lips released the claim he had on her. But he didn't move. His forehead rested against hers. His arms encircled her waist. She could feel his heart pounding beneath his shirt and hear his ragged breaths.

"I shouldn't have done that."

His words slammed into her heart. No, he shouldn't have. And she shouldn't have let him. What had she been thinking? She stepped back, knowing she had to flee before he saw her tears. "I've gotta go."

"Julianne—"

She hurried toward the door, not stopping to look back… or say anything. Escape. That's what she had to do.

Before he could call out to her again, she slammed

the door, ran downstairs and locked herself in the small apartment.

Not even her fears over being in danger could distract her from the deep pain of humiliation she felt. She pulled her knees to her chest and fought the despair that threatened to swallow her.

EIGHT

Bradley ran a hand over his face as he stood in his empty living room. When Julianne fled, she seemed to take all of the life and energy out of the room with her.

What had just happened? What had he been thinking?

One moment he'd been so intent on keeping Julianne at arm's distance. The next moment, he'd seen the scar. He'd known that something terrible had happened to her, and his heart had twisted with compassion.

More than compassion.

His heart had welled with protectiveness. Fierce protectiveness. Had Darrell done that?

He turned around, resisting the urge to punch something. He'd blown it big-time. All he'd intended to do was comfort her, but instead he'd sent Julianne running for cover. And his bold proclamation that he "shouldn't have done that" hadn't helped anything.

But he *shouldn't* have done that, no matter how sweet the moment had felt. He had no business kissing her. They had a professional relationship and nothing more.

He knew that wasn't exactly true, especially not at this very moment. He'd been trying to keep his emotions at bay since the woman had shown up at the Eyes headquarters. His feelings had taken over his senses for a moment—a very enjoyable moment.

He paced the living room. He should go downstairs and try to talk to her. No. He shook his head. He needed to give her space. And the truth was, *he* needed space before he did something else he regretted.

A relationship with Julianne was out of the question for more than one reason.

He sat at the kitchen table, turning his focus instead on something he was good at—his job. He reviewed what had happened tonight.

If those men had wanted to kill Julianne, they could have. So why didn't they? What did they want from her? Someone had shot the thug who'd been trying to grab Julianne, and it hadn't been Bradley. He'd been on the other side of a boathouse when it happened. Had Darrell—or the person imitating Darrell—fired that shot? Was he trying to kill Julianne or protect her?

Of course, the big question was: Who were those

men? Could one of them have been Darrell's best friend, Tommy Sanders? The idea carried enough weight that Bradley decided he would track down Tommy and ask him a few questions tomorrow.

And what about the caller who'd taken a little too much interest in Julianne? Was there any way to find him?

But an even bigger question still nagged at him. Diane had disappeared before Julianne arrived. What if all of this had something to do with Bradley and not Julianne? Had she become some kind of pawn in a plan to hurt him?

He rubbed his temples, the answers seeming too far out of reach for his comfort.

Julianne curled up on the couch and took a deep, calming breath.

What had just happened? How could Julianne have allowed a kiss to take place? The last thing she wanted was to be romantically involved with anyone. The even scarier part was that she actually found herself enjoying the kiss for a moment.

She couldn't do that. No. There were too many similarities between Bradley and Darrell. She was dependent on both of them. Striking out on her own seemed impossible without money or a car. Just like with Darrell. But there were differences, also. Bradley would never hurt her...would he?

She had to stop thinking that every man was like

Darrell. But that was easier said than done. It was why she hadn't dated anyone since Darrell's funeral, right? She found trusting men to be next to impossible. That was why she'd vowed to remain single. Better single and independent than with the wrong man and miserable.

A knock sounded at the door. "Julianne, it's me, Bradley. Detective Spencer needs to speak with you."

The detective. Of course. How could she have forgotten what happened? "Just a second." She dragged herself from the couch, threw on a clean sweatshirt and quickly ran a brush through her hair. Before turning the doorknob, she drew in a deep breath, a last-minute attempt to compose herself.

She pulled the door open, careful not to make eye contact with Bradley as he slipped inside. She waved toward the table, and the detective sat there. She lowered herself across from him, all too aware of Bradley's presence beside her.

Detective Spencer opened his ever-present notebook. "I heard you had an unfortunate encounter down at the oceanfront."

She recounted what had happened. As the man's voice and smell came back to her, she shivered. That had been close. Too close. And if Bradley hadn't been there…she didn't even want to think about what would have happened.

"Julianne, do you know anything about the Amigos?"

She shook her head. "The Amigos? I can't say I do."

"They're a Mexican drug cartel that's infiltrated the U.S. at a rapid pace within the past five or so years. They're not a group that you want to mess with. They're dangerous and take no prisoners, so to speak."

What was the detective getting at? She rubbed the table with her finger, trying to get out an imaginary stain. "They don't sound like a group I'd want anything to do with."

The detective shifted. "One of the waitresses saw what happened tonight. She said she saw a certain tattoo on the man who grabbed you. The tattoo is of three hands huddled on top of each other. The symbol is nearly always affiliated with the Amigos."

Of all the scenarios Julianne thought she might hear, a Mexican drug cartel never even entered her mind. She continued rubbing the invisible stain, the motion somehow helping her to process her thoughts. "So a member of the Mexican cartel tried to grab me tonight? Why in the world would they do that? I've never touched drugs. Not even cigarettes."

The detective leaned back, clicking his pen

closed. "That's what we're trying to figure out. Do you deal with any of them in your line of work?"

"I wouldn't know. All the calls I take are anonymous." She shook her head. "This just keeps getting weirder and weirder. I have no idea."

Detective Spencer stood and gripped his notebook. "Thanks for your help. And be on the lookout. I don't know what's going on, but I do know that you seem to be the target."

Bradley walked him to the door and gently shut it as he left, clicking each of the locks in place. Now it was just the two of them.

Why was her heart pounding erratically?

Bradley paced until he was beside her. She could feel his presence. Each of her hairs seemed to stand on end. Her skin prickled. Her heart raced. It had been a long time since a man had that effect on her.

"Julianne, about what happened upstairs…" He lowered his head, and his voice sounded soft and husky.

She shook her head. "Let's just forget about it."

"It shouldn't have happened. I was out of line." She could hear the sorrow in his voice. Sorrow over kissing her. Yes, she understood. Their emotions were amped. Stress could cause people to act in strange, oftentimes impulsive ways.

She nodded, really wishing he'd leave so she could be alone. Except a part of her wanted him to stay. A part of her wanted to have someone there to comfort her. Why were her emotions such a tangled mess? "Don't worry about it, Bradley. I've… I've forgotten it already."

He stayed quiet for a moment before turning away. "I'm turning the alarm system on, so don't open the door or windows. I'll be down to check on you in the morning. It's Saturday, so I won't be going into Eyes to work, though I probably will do some work here at home."

She nodded again.

He paused by the door, as if he wanted to say something else. Finally, his chest rose as he took a deep breath. He nodded and stepped outside.

And again, Julianne felt alone, as if there was no one within sixty miles of this place whom she could rely on.

She curled up on the couch again and opened her Bible, just as she always did when her thoughts started to overwhelm her.

She found Psalm 9:9. *The Lord is a refuge for the oppressed, a stronghold in times of trouble.*

No, there was someone she could rely on, no matter where she was.

God.

She closed her eyes and repeated the verse over and over.

The next morning, with Julianne safely tucked inside his house and the alarm set, Bradley donned his running shorts and sneakers. He paused by his front door. "I'm going out for a run. Are you okay with that?"

Julianne looked up from the couch where she'd been doing Sudoku puzzles for the past hour. "Of course."

"Keep the alarm on and the doors locked until I get back. No exceptions."

"No problem." She stood and stretched, her trim, athletic form nicely filling out the jeans and sweater she wore. She walked over to the door—toward him—and waited until he stepped out. He paused outside until he heard the locks click in place and the beep of the alarm. Good girl.

He'd be gone only a little while, and he'd be close enough to help her if she needed it.

When he got stressed, nothing seemed to help him sort out his thoughts like a good run. The wind whipped around him, downright cold as it grazed over the waters of the Atlantic. He didn't care. The briskness would only push him to run faster and farther.

He'd had another sleepless night. There was too much on his mind, and none of those things were the project he was supposed to be working on. No, instead his thoughts were on Julianne and her scar…and their kiss. Things that he had no business thinking about.

Too many thoughts were crashing together in

his head, including his sudden, overwhelming feelings for Julianne. He hadn't been attracted to someone like this since he'd been engaged. But, even if circumstances were different, was he ready for a relationship? He didn't know the answer to that question. His mind told him no, but his heart told him yes.

And the questions didn't stop there. Why would a member of the Mexican drug cartel go after Julianne? Was that really what this was all about? Or did it all come back to Darrell? Could he actually be alive…or was someone else simply trying to make it look like he was? Who would do that?

He ran along the shore, close enough to the water for the sand to be packed at his feet but far enough away that he didn't get sprayed by the ocean's massive waves. The salt air always relaxed him. Each pace helped him to sort out life and burned away some of his anxiety.

Movement in the distance caught his eye and caused him to slow. Was that a person up on the sand dunes lining the beach? A vacationer maybe? A beach resident doing some bird watching? His gut told him that neither of those guesses was correct.

A gun rested in the holster beneath his sweatshirt. He almost hadn't brought it, but he had at the last minute, especially as he remembered the events from the previous evening. Better safe than sorry. Looked as if that precaution may work in his favor.

His gaze scanned the shore again. Nothing. Where had the figure gone? Bradley was sure he'd seen someone hiding behind the tall grasses of the dunes. He slowed his pace.

Mexican drug cartel? Darrell? Someone imitating Darrell? He wasn't sure which was worse. Of course, he'd prefer none of the above. He'd prefer to go back to his life as it was four days ago.

But then he would have never run into Julianne.

Out of the worst circumstances also came the most beautiful things. Wasn't that the way life often worked? But he couldn't fool himself. Even though he was attracted to Julianne, a relationship between them would never work. He still mourned the loss of Vanessa. Besides, he was married to his job, and Julianne seemed anything but interested in a relationship. In fact, she'd even said she desired to remain single.

He could respect that. In fact, if he kept her wishes in mind, it would make their time together more comfortable. He'd just have to forget about the attraction that flickered between them. Separating his actions from his emotions was something he prided himself in.

He ran a few more steps before turning around, ready to head back to his house. Something popped in the distance. Bradley recognized the sound.

Gunfire.

He sprinted toward the dunes, desperate for cover. Out by the breaking waves, he was an easy target with nowhere to hide.

Another pop sounded and something whizzed past his shoulder. He grabbed his gun from beneath his sweatshirt and rolled on the ground out of the line of fire. He scanned the area around him, looking for cover.

A walkover would provide just the shelter he needed. He pulled himself to his feet, ready to dart toward the structure. Twenty feet. He could make it that far. A line of bullets hit the sand at his feet as he ran. He had to get there in time. Had to.

Another bullet buzzed past, grazing his arm. This guy wasn't playing games. Someone was out for blood.

Bradley reached the walkover and hunkered down behind it, his gun drawn. Pain trickled from his arm, but he ignored it. He waited. What would the shooter do next? Get closer? Continue shooting until he either ran out of ammunition, or hit his target?

A head full of dark hair breached the sand dune. The shooter? Could it be him? The man was too far away, and he'd ducked back down before Bradley could get a good look at him.

He grasped his gun, too familiar with how to use it. Bradley didn't want to fire. There were too many uncertainties. At any moment, someone could stroll down the beach with their dog or with a Frisbee.

He didn't want to fire, but he did want to catch the perpetrator so he could finally put an end to this reign of terror. Staying behind the walkover, he crouched down and made his way toward the street. An older woman with a poodle started his way. "Get back inside," he hissed. The woman's eyes widened and she scrambled back toward her beach house.

Another bullet dug into the sand only feet away. Whoever this guy was, he was brazen. He didn't care who got in the way. Nothing was going to stop him from accomplishing whatever it was he wanted to accomplish. Was that to scare Julianne? To kill anyone who got close to her? Then why had Diane disappeared? Was she connected to this? He'd have to ponder that later. Right now, he had to stay alive.

What had that caller said on the hotline yesterday when Julianne answered? That Bradley was next? What kind of threat was he in connection to Julianne?

He finally made it to the street. His gaze scanned the road, but beach houses blocked any views of the shooter. He crept forward, sheltered by the houses, but still rigid and on guard as he waited for the sound of the next pop.

No bullets. But at any time now another one

could rip through the air. Was the gunman watching him now? Did he have Bradley in his crosshairs?

He slunk behind a car for a moment to take in his surroundings. Where had the man gone? He didn't see a sign of anyone suspicious, but that didn't mean anything.

Suddenly the sound of a motorcycle revving its engine filled the air. He raised his head in time to see the same bike from two days ago squealing down the road.

He raised his gun to shoot at a tire when another movement caught his eye. A little girl running out to check the mail, oblivious to the danger around her. Bradley lowered his gun.

The gunman had gotten away. Again.

He brushed the sand from his legs. Heaviness pressed on his chest.

One day, he was going to catch this guy. Just give him time.

Julianne paced by the door. Where was Bradley? What was taking him so long? Should she go out and look for him? Or were the events of the past week simply wreaking havoc on her emotions and making her paranoid? Or maybe it was the phone call she'd just received....

Sorrow pounded in her heart as she glanced out the window again. This time, she spotted someone walking toward the house. As customary lately, her muscles tensed. Was it Bradley? Or someone else, someone she should be worried about?

Stomping sounded on the stairs. Finally, Bradley's face came into view. She let out the breath she held.

Until she saw the blood gushing from his biceps.

Her heart quickened. What had happened? Was he okay?

She waited until he was at the door to punch in the numbers for the alarm and let him in. Her eyes quickly assessed him. Perspiration dotted his brow, his sweatshirt was ripped and dirty, and blood stained his sleeve.

"Are you all right?" She started to reach for him but stopped herself. She had no right to touch him. So why did she feel like she did?

"Someone was shooting at me." He locked the doors and set the alarm again before turning back toward her. "I don't know what's going on, but I don't like it."

"You're hurt…."

He shrugged, as if this happened to him every day. "The bullet just grazed my skin. Nothing the first-aid kit can't handle."

"Let me get it for you." She hurried down the hallway before he could object. She'd seen the kit in the bathroom earlier when she'd been cleaning. She had to do something to pass the time, so cleaning had seemed like a good option. She grabbed the plastic box from underneath the sink and jogged back to the living room.

Bradley already had his sweatshirt off and his sleeve rolled up. The cut slashed across his biceps, probably two inches long. He was right. It wasn't deep, but it did need to be cleaned.

Flashbacks from last night flooded her mind. The memory of their kiss made her cheeks flush. That should have never happened.

"You should sit." She prodded him into a kitchen chair without too much resistance. But as she put antiseptic on his wound, her throat felt dry as she noticed the tautness and definition of his muscles. He definitely worked out, and it showed in his physique. She'd known that before, but now that she was touching his arm and soaking him in without reservation, his potent masculinity hit her twofold.

She cleared her throat, trying to concentrate on the task at hand. Which was easier said than done because it required her to look at that incredibly muscular biceps.... If he noticed her flustered state, he didn't give any hints of it. Using a piece of gauze, she patted the cut dry and placed a bandage over it. "All better."

He rolled his sleeve down and stood, obviously unaffected by her nearness. He'd put yesterday behind them, and that was a good thing, no matter how much her heart tried to tell her otherwise.

Bradley took a step away. "Thanks. I need to call the detective and tell him what happened."

She cleared her throat again. "Actually, he called while you were out."

Bradley turned toward her, his eyes widening with curiosity. "And?"

Julianne shifted, unsure how to break the news. There was no easy way to say it. "Bradley, they found Diane."

"What happened? Is she okay?"

Julianne shook her head, sorrow pulling down her lips into a frown. "She's dead, Bradley. I'm so sorry."

He closed his eyes and hung his head as regret washed over him. "I can't believe it." He sat down.

Julianne sat beside him and laid a hand on his arm. "It gets worse. At the crime scene, there was an energy drink container and seafood-flavored potato chips wrapper."

NINE

Julianne watched as Bradley raised his head. His strained gaze met hers. "Tell me what Detective Spencer said."

Julianne felt the tension flare between them. Was Bradley blaming her for his secretary's death? She put the thought aside. She'd never even met the woman. Still, guilt trickled into her conscience. "A jogger found her body in the woods this morning at that park off of Dam Neck Rd. She'd been shot."

Bradley's eyes flashed with something Julianne couldn't read. "Off of Dam Neck?"

"That's right."

He stood, the tension in the room growing thicker as pain flitted across his face. His muscles looked pinched and a knot formed between his eyebrows as his eyes squeezed shut.

She wanted to reach out and offer a soft touch of support. But she kept her distance instead. "What's wrong, Bradley?"

"That park was…it was Vanessa's favorite place. She used to go run there every morning."

The moisture left Julianne's throat again as facts collided in her head. Her heartbeat felt heavy in her chest. "That can't be a coincidence."

He opened his eyes, his gaze focusing on her. "Did the detective say anything else?"

"He said that Diane was wearing a necklace that didn't belong to her." Julianne's face lost all of its color as realization started to spread through her. The park where his fiancée used to run. A necklace with a…

Her hand covered her mouth, covered the O of horror. She shook her head. The thought seemed incomprehensible. It couldn't be right. It couldn't. She couldn't tell Bradley the rest. She couldn't bear to see the look in his eyes. But she had no choice. Bradley watched her, waiting for the rest of the information. He deserved to hear the truth, no matter how much it might hurt.

"Julianne?" His hands went to his hips, the ever-present tension still there. Julienne could see where someone could be intimidated by his massive figure towering over them, but, surprisingly, Julianne felt no fear or anxiety over Bradley, only over what she had to tell him.

"I'm sorry, Bradley," she whispered, her voice breaking with every other syllable.

"Sorry for what? What aren't you telling me?"

She swallowed before sucking in a deep breath and daring to meet his eyes. "The necklace was a gold chain with a charm on it. A *V* charm." *V* as in Vanessa?

Bradley ran a hand over his eyes. His face lost all tautness and his shoulders sagged. "A *V* charm?"

"That's what the detective said. He asked me if I'd ever seen it before. I'm so sorry, Bradley." She took a step toward him and placed a hand on his arm. She'd vowed to stay away, but all she wanted was to be close.

His eyes closed again, grief evident. "I gave her that necklace. The police never found it after she was murdered. I just figured it had fallen off or gotten lost somehow."

"It looks like the same person who killed your fiancée killed Diane also. I'm so sorry, Bradley. So incredibly sorry."

Bradley's head felt as if it was spinning as he tried to connect all of the pieces. The sorrow on Julianne's face as she stood next to him, her hand on his arm, was nearly enough to do him in. The unbelievable facts surrounding the murder wouldn't quite settle in his mind, though.

He sat back down at the table and Julianne lowered herself across from him, her brows furrowed with worry. She laced her fingers together on the table and waited like a counselor might.

He shook his head, wishing the action would somehow make all of the pieces magically fall into place. "Somehow we're connected, Julianne."

"But Darrell's the only commonality we have."

Had Darrell killed his fiancée? Was that possible even? Was Julianne luring him into her delusion? He stood, not liking where his thoughts were going. He had to sort everything out, and he couldn't do that in his dining room with Julianne's luminescent eyes on him.

He stood. "I need to be alone for a moment. If you'll excuse me."

Before she could respond, he went upstairs to his office. The room overlooked the ocean and all of its glory. Right now, that didn't matter. Thoughts of his fiancée's murder flooded back to him with the same fury of those waves crashing on the ocean.

Someone had stolen Vanessa's necklace after they murdered her and waited until they killed Bradley's secretary to pull out the necklace again. There was no way that what was happening to Julianne and what was happening surrounding him weren't connected. The coincidence would be too big, too unbelievable.

He thought about the facts for a moment. First, Darrell supposedly dies in a training exercise. Then Vanessa is killed by an intruder. Someone claiming to be Darrell pops up again in Julianne's life. The Mexican drug cartel also shows up. Bradley's secretary is killed and left with a morbid reminder of his fiancée's death. All of that happened while he was developing equipment for the Department of Defense, equipment that enemies from other countries would love to get their hands on.

What sense did all of that make?

It didn't. No matter how he looked it, it didn't make sense.

He stayed in his office, making calls to the detective and to Diane's family and to Jack Sergeant. At some point, a tantalizing scent drifted down the hallway and pulled him from his heavy thoughts. His stomach grumbled, reminding him that he hadn't eaten lunch yet. A glance at the clock told him it was way past lunchtime.

He stood, stretching. He never was very good at being around people when thoughts weighed heavy on his mind. He preferred solitude in moments like this. But something about the idea of being around Julianne right now appealed to him. Sometimes it would be nice to have someone to depend on, to share his life with.

Of course, on the other end of the spectrum was the realization that losing the people you loved seemed unbearable. When Vanessa died, his world had crashed around him, and it had been only his faith that helped him get through that time—his faith and his determination to find whoever took her life.

In addition to searching tirelessly for answers during those first six months, he'd also made a point of breathing down the detectives' necks to make sure they didn't drop the ball. He'd found leads, but nothing that had led him to the right suspect. Eventually, he'd tried to let it go. But in the back of his mind, that desire was always there— that desire for justice. Was he being handed another opportunity to find her killer? Would he finally be able to put her death behind him if he did?

He needed to talk to Julianne. He opened the door, and the scent of garlic and onions became stronger. When he stepped into the kitchen, his heartbeat quickened a moment. She stood at the stove, mixing something in a pot. Her hair was pulled into a sloppy ponytail. At once, he remembered the feel of her lips on his last night.

What would it be like if he were able to go up to her now and wrap his arms around her? What would it be like for this house to become a home, filled with warm family dinners and the patter of little feet?

It didn't matter. He couldn't do that. Even if he allowed himself, Julianne had made it clear that she had no interest.

She looked up. "I hope you don't mind. I decided to make some zucchini soup and some sandwiches."

"Zucchini soup?"

She tapped the wooden spoon on the side of the pot. "It's delicious. You'll love it. Guaranteed. My mom used to always make it for me growing up."

He smiled. "You didn't have to cook. We could have ordered in."

"I need to keep busy or I'll go crazy."

He sat down just in time for Julianne to set a steaming bowl before him, along with a thick sandwich piled high with lunch meat and veggies. A moment later, she sat across from him with her own food.

"Julianne, I have to admit that I didn't know what to make of your allegations when you showed up, but now I can't deny that something sinister's going on. I also can't deny that it somehow concerns me, as well. Truth is, I was connected to all this before you came around…but I just didn't know it."

Julianne's somber expression foreshadowed the words to come. "My fiancé wasn't a nice man, Bradley."

He set his spoon back down on his plate. He didn't want to bring the subject up, but he had to. "He gave you that scar, didn't he?"

She hesitated, her eyes focused on the soup bowl, before finally looking up and nodding. "I'd tried to break up with him and he flew into a mad rage. He showed up at my apartment a few hours later, acting like he was going to apologize and going into a long soliloquy about how he was going to change.

That was typical of him. He always had the most convincing reasons for his tirades. Sadly, I believed him." She shook her head. "But not that day. I'd believed him too many times already at that point."

"What happened next?"

Lips quivering, she released a deep, tremulous breath. "When I refused to accept his apology, he pulled out a bottle. I thought there was water inside. The next thing I knew, he unscrewed the top and threw the liquid at me. I moved right as he splashed me. Otherwise, the liquid would have hit my face."

He could see the strain on her features, from her tense shoulders to her watery eyes. "You don't need to finish."

"No…I want to." She furrowed her brows and then nodded as if deep in thought. "The contents of the bottle hit my shoulder. At first, it felt cold, like ice water. Then I felt the burning. It was searing, intense. I almost passed out from the pain. It was unlike anything I'd ever felt before. I could hear the sizzle on my skin. He'd thrown acid on me."

Bradley's eyes closed in disgust of what Darrell had done. His SEAL team had seen acid burnings while over in Afghanistan. They'd seen women disfigured by their husbands. Some had lost eyesight, others dignity. Some were so scarred that they committed suicide rather than face reality. Was that where Darrell had gotten the idea?

"Darrell meant the acid for my face. He wanted

to disfigure me so that no one else would ever want me. He almost got his wish." She shuddered at the memory. "I had second-degree burns in most spots on my shoulder. A few areas had third-degree burns. The physical scars will be with me forever, but I'm determined that my emotional scars will heal one day."

Anger boiled beneath the surface. No one should ever be treated like that. No one. "Did you report him?"

Tears glimmered in her eyes. "He was leaving the next week for training. He threatened that if I told anyone, he'd come back and wouldn't miss next time. He even took me to the hospital. I told them I was trying to unclog a drain and spilled the acid on myself. No one seemed to question it. I decided to wait until he was gone to report him, because it would give me the space I needed to get away. I went to the police, but he was already dead."

He stared at her, desperate to see beyond her words to the unbearable hurt that had obviously changed her. "What happened after you went to the hospital, Julianne?"

She shrugged. "After that he was on his best behavior for the next few days. Then he was sent to Arizona for the training. I knew that was my opportunity to get away. I was going to move, to not be there when he got back." She paused, turning toward him with an unwavering gaze. "I didn't have to do that, though. You showed up at my door."

"I can't imagine, Julianne. I'm sorry."

"I always thought I was stronger than all of that. But I wasn't. You get sucked in, one emotion at a time and before you know it, you're buried. Darrell was a great manipulator, and I fell for him." A hint of sorrow lingered in her eyes. "I've been getting counseling for the past year, trying to separate myself from the incident. I've been making progress. Until my counselor died, at least."

"Why were you so certain your counselor's death wasn't an accident?"

She shook her head and looked off in the distance. "Alan was such a safe person. He didn't take risks. And we were close. I mean, we didn't date, but we were friends. I think he would have liked for us to have been romantically involved, if things had been different, you know."

"And that was enough for you to think that Darrell did it?" He desperately wanted to figure out where her thought pattern had come from, especially now that her story seemed to have merit.

"I'd been receiving some weird phone calls. And I constantly felt like I was being watched. I even thought I saw Darrell once, but then I dismissed it, thought I was going crazy. When I saw the chip wrapper and energy drink, that's when I really got frightened." She spread out her hands. "And now all of this.... I thought I'd pulled you into this mess. It turns out, you were already there. I'm so sorry, Bradley."

The sincerity in her voice made his heart fill with some strange emotion. "Don't blame yourself. You're just as much a victim as anyone here."

"I just don't understand the connection, though. Why would Darrell kill your fiancée? I can't make sense of it."

His mouth flattened into a hard line. "I can't, either. But I'll get to the bottom of it. Even if it takes me years."

"We may not have years. I don't think he's going to back off until someone else dies." Her words held an edge of truth and reason.

And he knew Julianne was correct. They didn't have years. They may not even have days, because around every turn, someone was determined to send a clear message of "I want you dead."

An hour later, Julianne and Bradley cruised down the road. He'd informed her that they were paying a visit to Tommy Sanders. Since getting out of the military, he worked at a local firehouse. Bradley had called to make sure he was on duty today, and he was.

Julianne had always felt a bit weird around Tommy. Once when she and Darrell had been dating, Tommy had shown up at her apartment. He reeked of alcohol as he told her she was the most beautiful woman he'd ever met and that she should leave Darrell and date him instead. Of course, she'd dismissed him and sent him home. They'd never spoken about it since then.

They pulled to a stop in front of the modest building, and Bradley led her to the door. They stepped inside the truck bay where three fire engines were housed, and Julianne was relieved that Bradley was with her. He seemed to fill the space with confidence and ease and settle her nerves.

A man in work pants and a white T-shirt wandered over to them, and Bradley asked to see Tommy. A moment later, the former SEAL stepped into the room. He walked with the same cocky gait that he always had.

Bradley extended his hand to him. "Tommy Sanders. It's been a long time."

Tommy grinned. "It sure has." He shifted his gaze to Julianne. "Julianne, fancy seeing you again. To what do I owe the honor of this visit?"

"Is there a place where we could talk?" Bradley asked.

Tommy motioned for them to follow him into a small, sparse kitchen with an oak table at the center. They all took a seat around it. Julianne waited for Bradley's lead.

"Tommy, some strange things have been happening lately, and they all seem to go back to Darrell.

We were hoping you might answer a few questions for us."

He shrugged, but the action was so faint, it almost looked like a twitch. His arms rested on the table, and Julianne stared at his watch for a moment. It was a Luxor. She only knew that because she'd seen them on a TV show that had mentioned that the pieces cost twenty thousand dollars each. How did a firefighter afford that? "Sure thing. What can I tell you?"

"Has anyone claiming to be Darrell contacted you recently?"

Tommy's eyes widened. "Someone *claiming* to be Darrell?"

"I know it sounds strange, but it's like someone trying to bring him back to life, per se." Julianne pleaded with him, "Please, anything would help."

He looked from side to side as if contemplating what he might say. "I can't think of anything…"

Julianne swiveled closer. "Tommy, that day I ran into you at the restaurant, you seemed uncomfortable. Why was that?"

He raised his hands, as if he were being attacked. "I don't know what you're talking about."

"Your body language says you do." Bradley stared at him from across the table.

Tommy shook his head before drawing in a deep breath. "It's like this. I was on a date with one of the ex-girlfriends of a guy here. I was trying to keep everything on the down low. If I acted strange, it had nothing to do with Darrell."

Julianne watched him a moment. His gaze remained steady, and he didn't show any nervous twitches. He was probably telling the truth, she realized.

Bradley leaned forward, that piercing gaze still present in his eyes. "Did you get a letter from Dawn Turner recently?"

"Dawn Turner? Holden's wife? No. Why?"

"Just wondering."

Julianne's mind raced. Why had Bradley asked that? And why hadn't Tommy received the same letter? She shoved those questions aside, knowing she needed to deal with them later.

Tommy licked his lips. "Listen, since you're here…I wasn't going to mention this because I thought my eyes were just playing tricks on me. The other day, I was at the mall. I could have sworn I saw Darrell in the crowd. I looked for him again, but he was gone. That's crazy, right? Darrell is dead."

Bradley and Julianne glanced at each other.

The web surrounding Darrell was getting stickier and more tangled by the minute.

TEN

"What did you think of our conversation with Tommy?" Julianne asked as they left the fire station and cruised down the road.

"I think he's telling the truth about Darrell. But I also think he's hiding something."

"Did you see his watch? It was a Luxor. It cost more than I make in six months of work."

Bradley's eyebrows shot up. "Interesting. I wonder where he got that kind of money."

"I wonder that also. And why would you wear it to work if you were a fireman? If he's called to a fire, it could get ruined."

Bradley pulled to a stop in front of a warehouse. "Excellent question."

Before he couldn't change the subject, Julianne dove into her next question. "Bradley, why did you ask about that letter from Dawn Turner?"

He shrugged. "Just a hunch."

"A hunch?"

"It just seems odd that she would send that letter. I haven't heard anything from her in months. I didn't get the letter, and neither did Tommy."

"You don't think I made it up, do you?" she asked, narrowing her eyes.

He shook his head. "No, but I am going to dig a little deeper. Something's not sitting right with me about the whole letter thing." He gestured toward the building beside them. "I hope you don't mind, but I've got to run inside and pick up something. Come with me. Please."

She nodded, having no desire to stay in the car by herself. Not with everything that had been happening lately, at least. She quickly caught up with him, her gaze roaming the area as they hurried inside. Would there ever be a time when she didn't feel as if she had to watch behind her? She stepped closer to Bradley, tension strapped across her back.

They slipped inside an industrial-looking building where Bradley chatted with a man in a suit. He then picked up a box, signed it out and stuck it in the trunk. Ten minutes later, they were cruising down the road again.

She'd overheard snippets of the conversation while inside the warehouse and was more curious than ever about what was going on. "Am I being too nosy if I asked what we just picked up?"

"It's a prototype of a new explosive we're developing." He stared straight ahead, his gaze never leaving the road.

Julianne leaned back into the seat. A prototype. It must be pretty important if Bradley picked it up himself instead of sending someone else. She bit her lip, trying to think for a moment about something other than the person trying to kill her. "What exactly do you do, Bradley?"

"I develop new technology that we sell to the Department of Defense."

"Interesting."

"My uncle was a brilliant man. Truly. He had all of these ideas for equipment that the military could use. He even developed some new camouflage for the troops that would help them remain unseen. He had a few of his ideas developed before he died. I'm working to finish developing the rest of them."

"Tell me more."

"He died three years ago from cancer. I knew as soon as my term ended with the military that I wanted to get out and finish his work. Jack asked me to come on at Eyes."

"Wouldn't you make more money if you did it on your own?" she asked.

He nodded. "I would, but it isn't about money. It's about saving lives. Besides, Eyes provides the overhead I need to really develop the projects."

"It must pay well for you to have the house you do." It was none of her business. She knew that. But curiosity got the best of her.

"My uncle actually left that to me. The camo he

developed made him some big money. The house was his parting gift."

Julianne couldn't imagine having that kind of money. She'd always lived a modest life. "Did your uncle have a lot of other ideas he was developing?"

"A filing cabinet full."

"I bet you keep that under lock and key," she mused.

"You better believe it."

She leaned back into the seat again, trying to relax and feel normal. She doubted either of those would be her reality for a long time, though. "So what exactly did we pick up today?"

"Two things. The first is some new bulletproof clothing that's a lot more flexible and comfortable to wear and quite a bit more effective than everything else out there on the market. The second is a new device we're developing for explosive breaching, actually."

Surprise washed over her. "Explosive breaching? Really?"

He glanced over at her and nodded. "After Darrell died, I knew this was the next project I wanted to work on. I wanted to make it safer for our guys."

She turned toward him in the car. "Bradley, could you walk me through what happened that day that Darrell died? I mean, is there any possibility he is alive?"

"I don't see how he could have survived, Julianne. I really don't. He would have had to have a body double hiding at the training facility and he'd have only seconds to swap it out. Planning something like that, he'd have to be meticulous."

"He *was* meticulous."

He glanced at her again. "I was on the scene not even two minutes later."

"Two minutes would have been long enough for him to drag another body over, right?"

He hesitated.

Julianne could sense there was something he wasn't saying. "What?"

"There was about ten seconds where the video feed went down. It was right before Darrell set off the explosives." He glanced at her before looking back at the road. "I was watching the operations from a control room. It always bothered me that the feed went down, but sometimes with technology you just never know what's going to happen."

"Ten seconds? That was enough time, Bradley. He could have dragged a body double over— someone who was homeless or who wouldn't be missed—and then set off the explosion."

"There was an autopsy."

"Darrell was a smart man, Bradley. Too smart for his own good." She rested a hand on his arm as they pulled up to the beach house. "I know his death—or supposed death—still haunts you."

Mutual understanding passed between them.

"Come here. Let me show you something." He opened the car door, gesturing for Julianne to follow him out. Then he popped the trunk open and pulled out one of the prototypes from the box. It looked like a thick, black plastic bag, and wasn't any bigger than her hand. "This is what we've developed. You stick this bag on the door handle, light this fuse and you have five seconds to get away before it ignites."

"That sounds amazing."

"I have a great team that's helping me to develop these projects. I just want to keep our troops out of harm's way."

Julianne smiled softly. "Sounds like a noble calling, Bradley. It really does."

Despite her heart's resistance, she was starting to understand why so many people looked up to the man she'd once thought of as a stoic, stone-cold statue.

That evening, Julianne flipped through TV stations while Bradley sat in another chair reviewing some papers for his upcoming project. She'd spent the rest of the afternoon cooking and cleaning and doing anything else that she could to occupy herself. Soon, she'd have to go down to her own apartment and get some sleep, but, for now, she treasured the security of being around Bradley.

A rapping noise cut through the air. The door. Someone was at the door.

Bradley stood, his hand out and sending a clear "stay back" message. He crept toward the door when a deep voice cut through the air. "Bradley, it's Jack and Rachel. Denton and Elle are on their way up."

Bradley opened the door, and the couple strode inside, blankets in hand. Jack was tall and broad with chiseled features, and Rachel was a pretty brunette with petite features and a wide smile.

"It's bonfire night," the woman said as she extended her hand. "I'm Rachel Sergeant, and this is my husband, Jack."

Julianne rose to meet her. "Julianne. Nice to meet you."

Rachel turned back toward Bradley. "I know you have a lot going on, and I also know that you probably forgot about our plans for this evening. But we figured you could use the distraction."

Jack Sergeant stepped forward. "We figured we should be able to hold our own pretty well, even with everything that's been going on."

"Even people in danger need to have a little fun." Rachel's voice sobered. "Believe me. I've been there." Her gaze focused on Julianne, compassion clearly shining from the depths of her brown eyes.

Fun? The chance to forget—even for a minute— about everything that was going on? The idea had its appeal. Come to think of it, when was the last time Julianne could say she'd had fun? Probably not since before she'd met Darrell. Life had changed then, and not for the best.

Julianne glanced at Bradley to determine his feelings, and she saw hesitation in his deep breath, in the way his hands were stuffed into his pockets. "You're right. I'd forgotten that I'd said we could have a bonfire tonight. But as you mentioned, Rachel, there's a lot going on. I'm not sure it's a good idea…"

The pretty brunette grabbed his arm and shook him, the action playful but not flirty. "Don't back out on us now, Bradley. We even got a babysitter for the night."

Another couple walked inside, the man with a bit of a bad-boy appeal with his shadow of a beard, rakish grin and twinkling eyes. The woman with him was strikingly beautiful in a very classic way. Elle Philips, Julianne remembered.

Elle smiled warmly. "Julianne, this is my fiancé, Mark Denton. Sorry to barge in on you guys."

Bradley shifted again. "You guys are always welcome here. You know that. I just want to make sure you're all safe."

Mark Denton nodded toward the beach. "Jack and I scanned the perimeter before we came upstairs. We also brought some guys with us to keep an eye on things. Always prepared." He held up two fingers in a Boy Scout pledge. "That's our motto."

Bradley turned toward her. "You comfortable going down there?"

"If you guys say it's safe, then sure. Getting out of the house would be nice." It seemed strange to hear those words leave her mouth, especially since she was usually such a homebody. But it was one thing to stay inside because you wanted to, and an entirely different thing to stay inside because you had to.

Rachel smiled. "Great. Then we'll get things going and you guys meet us down there when you're ready."

Julianne grabbed some blankets and a stocking cap and slipped on her sneakers. A few minutes later, they were walking across the dunes, cold winter air biting into them. A bright fire danced in the distance. Julianne didn't miss the way Bradley continuously scanned everything around them, always on the lookout for trouble. She couldn't shake the feeling that someone was always watching her, even right now. She scoped out the area also. Several beach homes had windows lit. The stars sparkled brightly and a full moon illuminated their path.

No signs of danger. So why did she feel so on edge?

They joined the group on the beach. The three

men gathered on the other side of the bonfire and, from the look of things, Bradley was filling them in on everything that had transpired. Meanwhile, Rachel and Elle were talking wedding plans. Elle's big day was coming up in three weeks, apparently. Julianne loved listening to the excitement in her voice, though she did feel bittersweet. She wished there was a possibility of falling head over heels in love, of planning her dream wedding with her dream man. Those fantasies had died a quick death, though. Her heart twisted at the thought. Usually, she didn't care that her hopes of having a happy, loving family had died. However, right now, those pent-up yearnings seemed to come flooding back to her. But, equally as strong was the memory of how ugly love could turn. Could she ever get past those feelings? She stared into the crackling flames, absorbed in her own thoughts for a moment.

The bitingly cold air was held at bay by the flames that warmed their skin. She draped a blanket around her shoulders to ward off any remaining shivers. The sand offered a nice cushion below her, and between the crashing waves and the crackling of the fire, nature's symphony was playing at full force.

"Are you holding up okay, Julianne?" Elle asked.

She nodded. "I'm alive, so I can't complain. Bradley has been kind in helping me out, especially until I can get back on my feet." She filled them in on the events that had transpired over the past couple of days. She even found herself sharing a little about her past with Darrell.

"Relationships aren't always easy, but don't let one bad one spoil the rest of them for you," Rachel advised.

"Once you find the right one, all those old bad relationships are worth it. Believe me. I know." Elle's gaze traveled across the fire to Mark Denton. Her eyes absolutely glowed with affection.

"I wish I could feel that sure. Of course, I have bigger worries at the moment."

Elle patted her arm. "You're in good hands. These guys are seriously the best at what they do."

"Besides, we like to call Bradley's house Fort Knox," Rachel chimed in.

"Why's that?"

"He has all of these high-grade hurricane shutters and a steal door that not even the Incredible Hulk could get through. We like to give him a hard time about it. He has a lot of his uncle's ideas on file in the house, though, so we can understand his reasoning. He wants to make sure the data remains safe."

Julianne soaked in the new information. There was still a lot she didn't know about Bradley Stone. The more she learned, the more impressed she became.

Mark Denton pulled out a guitar and started

strumming some old songs from the nineties. When he finished, the two other couples cuddled up under their blankets together. Meanwhile, she and Bradley sat a few feet apart, each with their own blanket.

Suddenly, Julianne felt awkward, like an outsider. Even worse, she couldn't stop wondering what it would be like to be snuggled under a blanket with Bradley with the fire blazing in front of them. She tamped down those thoughts, trying not to think about their kiss and the fleeting moments of tender affection that had passed between them. But were Elle's words true? Was all the risk worth finding one good relationship?

She doubted it.

Bradley scooted closer to her. Her heart quickened at his nearness. The firelight danced across his face, casting an orange glow over it.

His gaze soaked her in. As her teeth chattered, he tucked the blanket tighter over her shoulders. "You okay?"

She nodded, digging her hands into the sand beneath her. "Yeah, I'm fine. This is nice. Do you do it often?"

"Whenever we can. Not as much lately, though."

She wondered if that meant since his fiancée had died?

"It seems like you have a great group of friends, Bradley."

A hint of a smile curled his lips. "Yeah, they

are great. When you depend on each other to stay alive, you bond quickly. We all met while we were in the navy. Jack and Denton were stationed together as SEALs. I was with a different platoon, but we trained together and worked a couple of missions jointly."

Bradley scanned the area. Julianne noticed the tautness of his muscles and the creases around his perceptive blue eyes. Not even the crackling of the fire or the crashing of the waves would put him at ease.

"What's wrong?" Julianne shivered again, the feeling of unseen eyes still nagging at her.

"I feel like we're being watched." His gaze remained focused in the distance. "I don't see anyone, but who knows who's staying in those beach houses? Most of them are rentals, so it could be anyone. I have only a couple of neighbors who actually live at the beach year round."

His words stayed with her for the rest of the campfire. Despite the lighthearted banter from everyone around her, she remained on edge. She half watched the fire disappear into embers, and half watched around her, waiting for the unexpected to transpire.

The cell phone buzzed in her pocket. She'd just turned it back on earlier and sorted through some missed calls. A number she didn't recognize lit the screen. She tensed as she answered.

"Are you enjoying the bonfire, Julianne?"

Shivers scrambled over her skin. Bradley's eyes met her and she mouthed "Darrell" before pointing around them to indicate he was nearby.

She studied the shadows around her, hoping for some sign of movement to signal Darrell's location. "Where are you, Darrell? Why don't you come out and join us?"

He laughed, the sound chilling her blood. "I would love to do that, Julianne, but we both know how that would turn out."

She tried to keep her voice steady, to keep him on the line while the men searched for him. "Why are you doing this? I don't understand."

"I thought you'd given up a long time ago in trying to understand me."

"But I want to now. I want this to end." More than anything she wanted this to end. She wanted it so bad that her soul ached with longing.

"The only way it's going to end is with more people dead."

She closed her eyes as heaviness pressed on her chest. "Don't take any more lives, Darrell."

"I don't have a choice."

"You always have a choice," she reminded him.

"You have no idea. Just remember, I'm doing it all for you, Julianne."

"I don't want you to do it for me," she choked out. "I just want this to end."

The laugh on the other line made her blood go cold. "You were meant for me, Julianne. And you'll be with me. I'll make sure of it."

Bradley adjusted his tie the next morning. He hadn't got much sleep last night, even with an Eyes agent stationed outside his home.

After the phone call to Julianne last night, Bradley, Jack and Denton, as well as the other Eyes agents, had scoured every inch of the beach and the surrounding property for Darrell—or the person masquerading as Darrell—but came up with nothing.

Then Dawn Turner had called him back. She'd never sent a letter. That meant one of two things—either Julianne had made the letter up, which he didn't believe to be true, or someone else had sent that letter to Julianne for the express purpose of letting her know where Bradley worked. The latter seemed the best possibility, and the only rationale he could come up with was that someone had purposely led Julianne to him. But why would someone do that? What purpose would it serve to bring the two of them together?

Bigger than that, he wondered what Darrell—or the imposter—might do next. Why did he have a feeling that the man didn't want to kill Julianne, only scare her? It was everyone around her who seemed to be in danger. Despite that, Bradley wasn't going anywhere. Julianne needed someone to keep an eye on her until this storm passed, and he was just the man for the job.

Last night flooded back to him again. They'd all been having a good time around the bonfire, and experienced a moment of normalcy until that phone had rung. Darrell had wanted them to know he was there; he'd wanted them to play his game. Bradley remembered that the man had always scored high on IQ tests, and he had no doubt that Darrell was planning more. He wouldn't stop until he was either caught, or until he got his way.

He finished getting dressed and hurried downstairs. The day wasn't as brisk as the previous ones. What had the weatherman said? It would creep into the upper fifties today? He knocked at Julianne's door, and, when she opened it, it was obvious she hadn't gotten much more sleep than he had.

It didn't matter. She still looked gorgeous in a flowing brown skirt and beige cardigan set. "You ready?"

She nodded behind her. "Let me just grab a jacket."

They stepped outside a moment later and, instead of going to his car, Bradley led her to his deck. She glanced up at him, her brows furrowed in curiosity. "What are you doing?"

He took her hand. "There's something I want you to see."

They reached the top and turned toward the

beach. Bradley pointed to the shoreline and watched as Julianne's eyes lit up. "Are those ponies?"

He smiled softly. "Wild horses. Beautiful, aren't they?"

"I'd heard there were some in Virginia. I've just never seen them. I didn't think they were real."

"They're real all right. You see more of them when you go into Back Bay."

"Back Bay?"

He pointed to the south. "Nine thousand acres of untouched wildlife. No vehicles allowed. It's all between the ocean and Back Bay. Beyond Back Bay is False Cape State Park. It's absolutely gorgeous there. If circumstances were different, I'd take you."

If circumstances were different... Of course, if circumstances were different, they might not have ever seen each other again.

"That sounds nice. If anything, this situation has made me realize that I've locked myself away for too long. I want to make some changes as soon as this whole crazy situation is behind me. I want to start really living."

Did that mean she would open herself up to another relationship? Bradley didn't ask, but he did like the idea of making some changes in his life also. He'd been too obsessed with work, with finding Vanessa's killer.

They watched the horses for a few more minutes

until finally descending the stairs and climbing into Bradley's car. Julianne cleared her throat as they headed down the road to church. "As soon as possible, I need to contact my insurance company again about my car. I need to start figuring things out for myself and get out of your way. I never intended to be here or inconvenience you for as long as I have."

His heart seemed to slow to a sobering rate. "You're not inconveniencing me, Julianne."

She pulled her gaze from her lap. "I appreciate you saying that. I do. But I can't go on depending on you like this. You've got a life to live. I can't expect you to drop everything because I showed up."

"Julianne…" What did he say? He couldn't very well beg her to stay, even though that's exactly what he wanted to do. But her leaving was not a good idea. "I think you should work for me. I need a secretary, and you need a job."

She blinked up at him. "Work for you?"

The idea had come from nowhere, but now that he'd voiced it, he realized it was a good plan. "Until you can get back on your feet, at least. The pay is decent. I'll have to do a background and security check. Standard procedure for hiring, you know."

Her eyelids fluttered again. "That's nice of you. I still have no car or place to stay, though. And there's the small fact that my dead ex-fiancé seems bent on hurting everyone around me."

"Running away isn't going to solve that problem."

"Running away? I'd hardly be running away. Maybe coming here was running away. Returning home would be facing the music, so to speak."

"I just mean that, even if you're not here, I don't think Darrell's done with me. As I mentioned before, I think I was involved before you ever came here." *And if you left, I think it would be because your heart is doing things you don't want it to do.*

They stopped outside a steepled brick building. Bradley hurried around to the passenger door and opened it for Julianne. Before she stepped away, he touched her arm. She looked up at him, and all he wanted to do was kiss her again. Of course, he couldn't.

"Julianne, please don't go." His voice sounded low and raspy.

Julianne's eyes searched his as they stood mere inches apart. What was she thinking? Was she feeling the same things that he did?

After a moment of silence, she nodded. "Okay… but I've got to stand on my own two feet. I can't depend on you for everything. I won't get caught in that trap again."

He nodded.

"And I have to go back up to my apartment to pick up some things for work."

"I'll take you today," he offered.

It only seemed natural when they turned that his hand slipped to her waist. It didn't matter how he looked at it. He was falling for this woman, and he was falling hard.

Julianne was well aware—too aware—of Bradley's nearness during church. Every brush of their arms or accidental touch of their legs made Julianne's heart speed. She knew she was developing feelings for this man. The problem was, she didn't want to. She wanted to run back to her old life. Her safe life. Only her old life wasn't safe anymore. Come to think of it…her current life wasn't safe, either. So where exactly did that leave her?

As church ended, Bradley led her back to the car. Again, every cell of skin on her body seemed alive at his closeness. She wanted to groan out loud. How had she fallen for this man, so hard and so fast? It had to be circumstances playing with her emotions.

She gave him directions on how to get to her apartment. It would be a good three-and-a-half- or four-hour drive, depending on traffic. They grabbed some sandwiches from a local deli to eat on the way.

Bradley settled back into his seat as they began their trip. "What did you do before you worked for this hotline, Julianne?"

She brushed some stray crumbs from her dress. "I worked at an after-school program for at-risk children in Norfolk."

"That's what you were doing when you met Darrell?" He took a long sip of his soda.

She nodded. "I loved it. Those kids were great, and it was a wonderful opportunity to truly make a difference in their lives. All those kids wanted was someone to love them and give them attention and delight in their accomplishments, to help them navigate through the hard times. For one reason or another, most of them didn't get that at home."

"You quit because you moved to the D.C. area?"

"I quit as soon as Darrell left to train in Arizona. I knew I had to report him and then get away. The acid burn crippled me emotionally, you could say. All I wanted to do was hibernate by myself. Even when I thought Darrell was dead, I still felt like I couldn't trust people, like some basic instinct inside me had been broken."

"What he did to you would be enough to make anyone like that."

The compassion in his voice made her want to tear down the walls around her heart. She cleared her throat and focused on anything but Bradley. "I found a new job up in D.C. It didn't pay much. We were funded by grants and donations. I started writing the grants for the organization and figured out I was pretty good at that, so I took on some freelance grant writing and that helped to make ends meet. Most jobs in my profession don't pay well."

"I'm sure Rachel and Elle could use your help with grant writing since they both run nonprofits."

She wondered for a moment what it would be like to stick around, to get to know Rachel and Elle better, to be a part of their inner circle. *Focus, Julianne. Focus.* "I actually enjoyed grant writing more than I thought. But what I really love doing is helping people."

"So what would your dream job be?"

"Funny that you ask because I've been thinking about that a lot lately. I don't really know. I just know I like helping people sort out their lives. Maybe I'd like to work with battered women." Sighing softly, she pondered the thought. "I've been in denial for a long time, but that's what I was. It's who I still am, because I've carried the effects of it with me for a while now. Sometimes the best way to overcome the hurts in your own life is to help others with their pain and to show them Christ's love."

Julianne was surprised at how easily their conversation flowed for the rest of the trip. They talked about everything from movies, to sports, to family and food. Before she realized how much time had gone by, they were pulling off the interstate and up to her apartment building.

The massive brick structure was located in a cluster of other similar buildings in one of the more rundown areas of town. It wasn't an ideal location, but it was affordable and she'd convinced her landlord to replace the carpet before she'd signed her lease.

Bradley walked close as they hurried toward the door to her building. They stepped inside, and the smell of popcorn and Clorox saturated the stairwell that cut through the center of the complex. Julianne's place was located on the first floor. She pulled her keys out and faced the door as a heavy sense of trepidation fell over her.

The keys in her hands trembled so badly that Bradley took them from her and opened the door himself. When the inside of her apartment came into view, Julianne gasped and stepped back.

The place was a mess—completely ransacked. Someone had obviously been here and they'd been looking for something. But what?

"Stay there." Bradley pulled his gun out and stepped inside.

Shakes overtook her as she stood in the doorway, observing the mess inside. Drawers had been dumped. Her couch cushions had been sliced open. Her TV had been smashed.

Bradley reappeared a moment later. "All clear."

She stepped inside, grateful for Bradley's hand on her elbow. "I don't get it."

"There are a lot of things that don't make sense right now. Why don't you get the things you need while I call the police?"

She nodded and dodged the mess on the floor

to get to her bedroom. She shuffled through papers and broken vases and scattered clothing until she found some files she needed for work, her cell phone charger, several changes of clothes and some toiletry items.

When she stepped back into the hallway, a wave of sadness hit her. Why did she have a feeling that this would be one of the last times she set foot here? Would that be by choice or by force? She wasn't sure.

ELEVEN

Bradley kept one eye on his rearview mirror as he drove back to Virginia Beach. The police had shown up rather quickly, taken their statements, and then they'd gotten back on the road. An hour into the trip, Julianne had closed her eyes and her breathing had evened out. She'd fallen asleep, and Bradley had no intention of waking her.

He hated to think of Julianne living in such a rough area. Groups of people hung outside the apartments with beer in one hand and a cigarette in the other. They weren't the type of people you wanted to invite over for dinner. No, gang activity was rampant there and he'd bet most of them had a rap sheet.

Still, she'd done what she could to stand on her own two feet. He had to admire her for that. She'd done her best with her given circumstances. However, his mind ran through possible ways of keeping her from ever having to go back there to live again. Maybe she'd accept a position at Eyes permanently? Or perhaps Rachel or Elle could use her at their nonprofits? He didn't know anything for sure, except that the thought of her moving away caused a strange ache to pierce his heart.

He glanced in the rearview mirror. A black sedan followed them. Every time he switched lanes, accelerated or slowed, the sedan mirrored him. The dark glass on the car's windows didn't allow Bradley to see the driver.

Spontaneously, he pulled off the interstate and cut onto an exit ramp. He watched in his rearview mirror as the car zoomed past. Good. Maybe he'd lost them.

Julianne raised her head, blinking as if trying to gather her surroundings. "What's going on? Where are we?"

"Just a little detour."

"Detour? Why?" she asked drowsily.

"I thought there might be someone following us."

She suddenly gripped the armrest and pushed herself upright. "Did we lose them?"

"It looks like it. I'm going to keep my eyes open, though."

She yawned and rubbed her hands over her eyes. "I didn't mean to fall asleep."

"You must have needed your rest."

"That was probably the best I've slept in a couple of weeks." As soon as the words left her mouth, her cheeks filled with color. "I haven't felt very safe lately, I guess."

The sun had set now, and darkness surrounded the car. The nighttime would make it harder to see a vehicle behind them, but he hoped if he continued on the back roads it would be easier.

"What was your fiancée like, Bradley?"

Normally, he shut down when people wanted to talk about Vanessa. But, for some reason, he didn't mind talking about her with Julianne.

"She was spunky and animated. She had a good heart. She put up with me." He grinned.

Julianne laughed softly. "Big job, huh? How'd you meet?"

"Through a mutual friend."

"You were never married before?"

He cast a quick glance her way. "No. Why?"

"I bet women were knocking down your door to get dates with you."

"And why's that?"

He smiled when he saw the blush stain her cheeks again.

"Oh, come on. You're going to make me say it, aren't you?" She cast a knowing glance his way.

"Of course."

"You're good-looking—"

"You think I'm good-looking?"

She ignored him and continued. "Successful. Stable. You don't go out to the bars every night or have three different kids by three different mothers or have dirty magazines hiding in your bathroom."

"You looked in my bathroom?"

She shrugged. "I cleaned your bathroom. I was bored, you know."

His smile dimmed, and he shrugged. "I've never wanted to settle. I was waiting for the woman that would knock my socks off."

"And Vanessa did that." Her voice sounded soft, wistful almost.

How could he tell her that she was the type of woman he'd been waiting for? He couldn't. Not now, at least. He knew that she needed time and space, and he planned to give that to her.

"I'm not going to lie. My grief after losing her almost did me in. All I knew about her killer was that he wore a size twelve shoe, he carried a nine-millimeter gun and he got into my house with no sign of forced entry."

"Maybe she answered the door, thinking the man there worked for you."

He nodded stiffly. "I've thought about that before." He gaze traveled to his rearview mirror. A new set of headlights appeared. Could the person following them have gotten off another exit and managed to find them again? His shoulders tensed. It was a possibility. "There was a man arrested for some break-ins at other houses in the area. The police thought, at first, that maybe he was guilty, but he never confessed to it. All of the leads dried up."

Silence stretched. Finally, he exited the highway and pulled into the parking lot of a restaurant. He glanced over at Julianne. Light from a street lamp illuminated her soft profile as she stared out the window.

He cleared his throat. "Hungry?"

Her wide, doelike eyes met his. "Now that you mention it, yes, I am."

He glanced in the mirror again and saw that the car continued past. A black sedan. They were definitely being followed. But by who?

He kept an eye on their surroundings as he ushered Julianne into the chain restaurant. Even when they were seated at a table and ordered their food, Bradley kept his gaze trained outside the window. No sooner had the waitress set a side salad in front of Elle did he see the sedan pull back in. The driver remained inside.

"Is everything okay?" Julianne asked.

He placed his napkin on the table and stood. "Can you excuse me a moment? I need to take care of something."

Julianne rubbed her lips together as if stopping herself from asking the questions that wanted to escape. Instead, she gave him a jerky nod. Bradley crept outside and went around the opposite side of the building with his gun drawn. He hunkered down behind some cars until he reached the black sedan. Slowly, he moved along the side of the vehicle, crouched low. He reached the door and threw it open, his gun pointed at the driver.

"Would you like to tell me why you're following us?"

The man in the driver's seat blinked and threw his hands in the air. "Don't shoot. I didn't do anything."

The middle-aged man had a slight build, messy hair and an even messier car. He was white, wore a stained sweatshirt and had the remains of his dinner dangling from the unkempt hairs of his beard.

Bradley grabbed his arm. "Get out of the car. Now."

The man climbed out, his hands still raised and a tremor shaking them. "Just don't shoot me. Please. I have a family."

Bradley kept his gun concealed, so any of the cars zooming past on the highway wouldn't become alarmed. "Then start talking. Now."

His gaze went to the barrel of Bradley's gun. He swallowed hard and a layer of sweat appeared on his forehead. "I was hired to trail you."

"By whom?"

"I don't know." The man shook his head, his eyes pleading for mercy.

Bradley cocked the gun. "I said, by whom?"

"Honestly, I don't know. It was all done over the

phone. He paid me online." The man's voice rose in pitch.

"What were his instructions?"

"I had to follow both of you and call to give him updates on where you were."

"Why?"

"He didn't say. I didn't ask…it wasn't any of my business. I figured it was a cheating spouse or something. Those are most of the cases I'm hired for." He mopped his sweaty brow. "He paid me. He paid me well, almost double what I normally get."

Someone with money and a plan, Bradley noted. "Did the man have an accent?"

"No. He sounded normal. You know, American."

That ruled out a member of the Amigos and left, most likely, Darrell or someone pretending to be Darrell. "How many times have you called this man?"

"Every hour. He needed to know when you got closer to Virginia Beach."

Warning signals went off in Bradley's mind. What exactly was someone doing back in Virginia Beach? He didn't know. He just knew he needed to get back there. Now.

He pulled a zip tie from his pocket and secured the man's hand to the outside door handle. He wouldn't be going anywhere—not until the police got here, at least. As a final precaution, he took the man's keys and tossed them into a drainage ditch behind him. Bradley would call the police on the road.

He went inside the restaurant and motioned Julianne from the door. She hurried toward him. "What's going on?" Her eyes were wide with fear. She glanced back at the man muttering outside the black sedan.

"We've got to go. I'll fill you in on things en route."

Julianne's muscles had never felt as tight as they did while on the ride home. Why would someone— most likely Darrell—hire someone to trail them? He seemed more like the type to pursue them himself.

Unless he couldn't because he had something else to do.

The thought didn't bring any comfort.

They pulled up to Bradley's house. The car belonging to the Eyes agent still sat in the driveway. His silhouette could be seen through the window.

Bradley turned toward her. "Lock the doors. Don't move. Understand?" His tone of voice brooked no argument.

She nodded.

He pressed something into her hand. "Just in case you need it."

"A gun?" The metal felt hot in her hands. She'd never fired a weapon before. Never.

"Just pull the trigger if you have to, and only if you have to."

His hand still remained over hers. His touch brought an unusual amount of strength to her. "Don't you need it?"

"I have another one. I'll be fine."

Before he got out of the car, she grabbed his hand and he turned back toward her. "Please be careful."

His eyes softened for a moment. "I will."

His hand slipped away, and she missed it instantly somehow. As the door slammed, she hit the lock button and slid down in her seat, watching everything around her with heightened awareness. Bradley knocked at the window of the car in front of them. The next second, he opened the door and the man inside fell to the ground.

Julianne covered her mouth as her jaw dropped open in horror. Was he dead? What had happened to him? Fear churned through her.

Bradley motioned for her to call the police. Her fingers shook as she grabbed the phone from her pocket and dialed 911. As she told the operator what had happened, Bradley ascended the steps and disappeared from view.

She prayed, hard and fervently. Every instinct in her screamed that she should go help the agent on the ground. But she'd promised Bradley that she'd stay put. Sitting in the car made her feel helpless, though.

She gripped the door handle, torn between a promise and the need to help.

Lord, what should I do?

Bradley crept toward the front door. The hurricane shades, thick metal blinds that protected the windows in storms, had been pulled down over the windows. The door was ajar, though barely.

Someone had been here. The question was were they still here?

Cautiously, Bradley stepped into his house. Everything was silent around him. Eerily silent and still.

He scanned his living room, the kitchen and everything else within sight. Every sense was heightened. Nothing appeared touched, but he knew better. Someone hadn't broken in just for kicks. They'd broken in for a reason. A bomb? A surprise attack? He didn't know.

Slowly, methodically, he checked each room on the second floor. He saw nothing. No one. But the nagging feeling that he wasn't alone remained with him.

Had something been taken? Some of his files perhaps? Though they were kept under lock and key, someone might not have known that. They might have tried to locate them.

He climbed to the third story of the home where his office, two extra bedrooms and a storage room were located. The bedrooms looked untouched, so he proceeded toward his office. He pushed open the door.

The place was ransacked. The filing cabinet had been knocked over, the computer screen smashed, papers scattered everywhere.

What had someone been searching for? And if they were simply looking for something, what was the purpose of pulling down the hurricane guards?

He'd worry about that later. Right now, he needed to get back downstairs and check on Julianne. He prayed this hadn't been a ruse to simply get to her.

As he descended the stairs, his head swam. The trip must be taking a toll on him because he was suddenly feeling exhausted and sluggish.

He paused as he reached the bottom step. What was different since he was down here last?

He scanned the area, stopping at the front of the house.

He'd left the front door open, he realized. He was sure of it.

So why was it closed now?

What was taking Bradley so long? Was he okay? Exactly how long did she wait before going for help?

Julianne scanned her surroundings. The sand dunes appeared normal and untouched as a breeze carried away the top layer, sending it into a spray that skimmed the landscape. The wooden beach chairs still cozily faced the ocean, beckoning anyone around to come and sit. Even the curtains from her apartment downstairs still remained just where they'd been.

From her vantage point, she could only see the start of the stairs leading to the front door. Another staircase was hidden behind her apartment, off of the wraparound deck upstairs.

There was no movement, not even a stray biker or jogger.

What was off? Why did something feel so incredibly wrong?

Her gaze focused on a doorway off the back of her apartment. The utility room, the place where the gas furnace and water heater and some other HVAC stuff were located, she recalled. She hadn't been in the room. She'd had no reason to.

She paused.

That's what was different.

The door to that room was cracked, just slightly. Why would someone have gone in there?

An inkling spread through her, cold and hollow. A conversation she'd had once with Darrell fluttered through her mind. She'd caught him doing some research on the internet. He'd smiled vacantly when she asked him about his search results. But now all kinds of realizations and theories began to fester in her mind.

Dread pooled in her stomach. If her hunch was correct, she needed to check something out. Now.

She grasped the gun, the metal heavy and cold on her fingers. Her hand trembled. She could do this. She *would* do this. Her other hand went to the door handle.

Before she could second-guess herself, she opened the door. Adrenaline and fear surged through her as she took the first step away from the sanctuary of the car. She propelled herself forward, toward the utility room. Each step felt surreal. Her gaze scattered about the area, searching for an intruder just waiting to pounce. She saw no one.

She shoved the door open and stepped inside the small space. She bypassed the cleaning supplies and brooms and stray beach chairs, and went straight to the gas furnace.

Her gaze went to the pipes running up from the top of the unit and into the ceiling above. Was that a hissing sound?

The pipe leading into the ceiling looked bent, as if it had been tampered with. She couldn't be certain—she only had a hunch to go on—but she trusted her gut.

She grabbed a wrench from a nearby shelf and

found the gas meter shut-off value. The metal twist came off in her hands. There was no turning it off.

Realization spread over her. She had to get to Bradley. Now.

TWELVE

Bradley didn't like the alarms sounding in his head. What was happening? His hand went to the doorknob. He twisted it, but the metal wouldn't turn.

Using all of his strength, he rattled the door. It was stuck. Someone had jimmied the lock.

Footsteps pounded up the steps, followed by the sound of someone slamming their fists into the door. "Bradley, can you hear me?"

Julianne. Why had she gotten out of the car? He'd clearly told her to stay inside.

"Julianne, what are you doing?" His head whirled. Something was wrong. Seriously wrong.

"You've got to get out of there," she said, her voice rising urgently.

He rattled the door again. "The door's jammed. What's wrong?"

"Carbon monoxide. Darrell messed with the heater downstairs. If I'm right, the amount of gas pouring into your house right is astronomical. You've got to get out." Panic laced each syllable.

That would explain his sudden headache and nausea. What about his detectors—why weren't they going off?

Someone had tampered with them, he realized.

They'd closed the hurricane shades and jimmied the door so he couldn't get out. They'd thought of everything, hadn't they?

He desperately needed some fresh air. But the windows were all sealed. Pulling his shirt over his mouth, he staggered toward them. Using the last of his energy, he pushed the windows up. Maybe some air would creep inside through the thick shutters. Maybe...

Had Julianne said "astronomical"? That wasn't good. Wasn't good at all.

"Can you shoot the locks? Do something?"

He stared at the door, the very ones he'd ordered because they were bullet-proof and virtually impenetrable. "These are high-grade steel doors. That's not going to work."

"What will?"

How did he get out of this mess? The carbon monoxide would kill him. He didn't know how much time he had. He only knew that his head was heavy and his eyelids heavier. He couldn't let sleep claim him. He might not ever wake up if he did.

"Bradley? Are you still with me?"

"I'm here."

"Stay with me. You understand?" she pleaded. He leaned against the wall. Take the hinges off, he realized. That's how he could get out.

If only he had the energy to get the screwdriver he needed to do just that.

Julianne couldn't wait for the police to show up. Who knew how long that would take? Each moment that ticked by brought Bradley closer to death. She wasn't going to let that happen.

But how could she get past this door? Bradley himself had said it was impenetrable. It was meant to keep people out, not to trap them inside, though.

An idea hit her. It was crazy. She knew it was. But was crazy enough that it just might work. Could she really do this? Did she have any other choice?

Determined to give it a shot, she pounded on the door again. "Bradley, I'll be right back. Stay with me, okay?"

"I'm here, Julianne." His voice sounded waning. It didn't matter how strong a person might be. Carbon monoxide could claim the toughest soldier. "What are you doing?"

"I'll tell you in a minute."

She scrambled down the steps. Her gaze skittered around her. Was Darrell here? Was he watching from the distance, enjoying seeing the pandemonium around him?

She shoved the thought aside. With trembling hands, she took the car key from her pocket and popped open the trunk. She stared at the supplies waiting there. Supplies they'd picked up yesterday but had yet to drop off.

Could she do it? She drew in a shaky breath.

She was going to do it.

She grabbed the explosive-breaching supplies that Bradley had left there for the upcoming training. He'd shown her briefly how to use them. Now she had no other choice but to use them to open the door and save Bradley.

She ran back upstairs, her pulse pounding in her ears, her hands shaking uncontrollably. Who did she think she was that she could pull this off? She shoved the thoughts away. She could—and would—do this. Bradley's life depended on it.

Her fist hammered at the door again. "Bradley, how are you doing?"

"I'm here, Julianne. You should go. Get in the car and get out of here."

"Not without you."

"Julianne…"

"Listen, Bradley. I have some of your explosive-breaching packs. I need you tell me how to use them."

He paused. "It's dangerous, Julianne."

"I can do it. You said these are safer than the normal method."

"I don't want you to get hurt. The police should be here soon."

"It might be too late by then," she said, trying to keep the panic at bay. "Tell me what to do."

Another moment of hesitation seemed to pass. "Okay, here's how to start…"

He walked her through the process. She attached the sack, just as he instructed and double-checked to make sure everything was in place. Then she stepped back and looked at her handiwork. A sliver of fear zinged down her spine.

"I have to step away from the door, Julianne. The carbon monoxide will ignite."

She nodded, knowing that he couldn't see her. Maybe the action was for her own sake. "I can do this, Bradley. Go ahead and get away from the door. I'll be fine."

"Julianne…"

Her throat burned as she swallowed. "Just go, Bradley."

"I'm going. Be safe."

"Okay, here goes, Bradley." She squeezed her eyes shut. What if this didn't work? It had to. She couldn't think like that. She had to pull back the tears that threatened to escape. "Everything's going to be fine. Hold on."

Lord, watch over us.

She ignited the match, put it in the door and then ran toward the steps.

The door exploded, just as the police turned into the driveway, sirens blaring. Had Bradley really moved away from the door? Or had he passed out before he could? Would they find his lifeless body?

Julianne waited outside Bradley's hospital room as the doctors examined him. She'd been quickly accessed by a medic and given the okay. But Bradley had suffered carbon-monoxide poisoning, as well as a concussion from the blast.

Two familiar figures walked down the hallway toward her. Jack and Denton. She stood, but Jack lowered her back into the chair before sitting beside her.

"We heard what happened. How are you?"

She wrung her hands together, still shaken up. "I'm okay. It was close, though. Really close."

"We're glad you're okay." Denton stood in front of them, his hands on his hips. "What's the latest on Bradley?"

"I haven't been able to see him, but I heard he's stable." She drew in a deep breath of relief. "How about the other Eyes agent? The one stationed outside the house. Is he okay?"

Jack nodded. "He's fine. Just a concussion. All things considered, it could have been much worse." He turned toward Julianne. "I have to ask—how did you know? How did you know it was carbon monoxide?"

"I remembered a conversation I'd had with Darrell once. He was talking about how carbon monoxide would be the perfect way to kill someone. He even mentioned how you could rig a heater to increase the amount of gas being released and then seal up the person's house. Everything just clicked in my mind."

Jack nodded again. "Smart thinking. You probably saved Bradley's life."

A nurse paused in front of them. "I'm afraid visiting hours are up. They've actually been over." She tapped her watch. "You're all going to have to come back in the morning."

Panic spread over her—both from leaving Bradley and wondering where to go. If she couldn't stay at Bradley's, then where?

Jack turned toward her. "How about if you stay at Eyes Headquarters tonight? We have some guest quarters there where I think you'll be comfortable. You should be safe."

She wiped a stray tear of gratitude from under her eyes. "I hate to leave Bradley after everything that's happened…."

"He'll be okay. We're going to station someone outside of his room tonight." Jack stood. "We'll bring you back first thing in the morning. How does that sound?"

She sniffled. "That sounds great. I really appreciate it."

"Any friend of Bradley's is a friend of ours." Denton winked.

Friend of Bradley's? The description was strangely foreign yet oddly comforting at the same time. Even stranger was the fact that they felt like *more* than friends, a progression that seemed impossible only a few days ago.

Denton nodded toward the exit. "How about if I take you there now? You should get some rest, especially after everything you've been through today. I heard you're going to be teaching some explosive breaching training for us soon." He grinned.

His lightheartedness helped to dissipate some of the tension she felt. "Don't hold your breath," she said dryly. "That won't be happening any time soon."

Bradley had never seen a sweeter face than when Julianne stepped into his hospital room the next morning. She smiled softly as she made her way to his hospital bed. The woman looked as beautiful as ever, even with the dark circles under her eyes. Her wavy golden-brown hair had been pulled back into a ponytail and the sleeves of her sweatshirt were drawn over her hands.

"Hey there." He tried to think of something else to say to the woman who'd saved his life. That was all that had come out, though. He'd blame it on the pain medication.

She stood at his side, her countenance full of compassion and worry. That scent of daisies on a rainy day floated over to him, bringing with it the soothing feeling of contentment.

"How are you feeling?"

"Been better, but I'm doing much better than I was about fourteen hours ago."

She smiled again. "I'm glad. You gave me a good scare."

He'd underestimated whoever was behind this mayhem. The reminder caused him to pull his lips into a tight line, and the initial contentment he'd felt at seeing Julianne disappeared. "I'm supposed to be keeping an eye on you, but you saved my life last night, you know."

"It's all in a day's work." She grinned and patted his hand.

Electricity charged through him at her touch. He wished more than anything that he could pull her into his arms and give her a proper thank-you. That would have to wait until another time, though.

She nodded toward him. "You're all dressed and ready to go."

He'd changed first thing, thanks to the clothes that Denton had dropped by early this morning. "It was ridiculous to be kept here overnight. I'm fine."

"He's been telling me that for about twelve hours now." A nurse bustled into the room, scowling at Bradley. "The doctor signed your papers. You're free to leave. Just don't trample me on your way out the door."

"I would never." His lip curled in a grin.

The nurse, a tall and painfully thin brunette in her fifties, paused with her hands on her hips. "Don't tell me that. You've been beside yourself, champing at the bit ready to leave."

He held up his hands. "Okay. You're right. I admit it."

The nurse looked at Julianne, her lips pursed in annoyance. "Take care of him. And bless your heart for putting up with the man." She waved a finger at Bradley. "He's an ornery one."

Bradley didn't bother to explain to the nurse that there were lives on the line. He'd simply let her think he was difficult. Sitting back and relaxing in the hospital did nothing to keep anyone safe.

Julianne grinned. "I'll manage. Thank you." She took his arm. "Would you like me to push you out of the hospital in a wheelchair?" Her eyes twinkled.

"That's not a bad idea," the nurse piped in.

"I think I'll manage." He stood and nodded toward the door. "Come on. Lets get out of this place." Two more seconds in that hospital room, and he might lose his mind.

Finally, they walked down the hallway, comfortable silence falling between them. He cleared his throat. "The detective informed me this morning that the levels of carbon monoxide in the house were at sixteen hundred. Much longer and I could have died."

"Darrell must have kept the house locked up—airtight—and let the gas fill the space, knowing you'd return." She pressed the down button on the elevator.

"Then he rigged the door handle and messed with the battery back-up for the hurricane shades. He's a clever man. I'll give him that." Much more clever than Bradley had anticipated. The fact that Julianne had to explosively breach the door made it even more ironic. Darrell had a sick, twisted sense of humor, that was for sure.

"Dangerously clever." Her words sounded somber as the elevator dinged and they stepped inside. "So now what?"

"We can't go back to my place, obviously. Jack gave us permission to stay at Eyes until we get things figured out." Speaking of Jack, Bradley spotted him at the hospital entrance after they exited the elevator. "He brought me here this morning," Julianne explained.

Jack nodded at them as they approached. "One of our guys drove your car here for you." He shoved some keys into Bradley's hand. "You're okay to drive, right?"

"Absolutely."

Jack clamped his hand on his arm. "Be careful, then. I don't like the way this is going."

"You and me both."

They drove back to the Eyes headquarters, and Bradley went straight to his desk. Julianne stood behind him. "What are you doing?"

"I have security cameras outside my home. All the video feed is sent to a website. I'm going to access the feed from yesterday and find out exactly what went down."

A moment later, the website came up. He typed in the time and date, and a video of the outside of his house came up. Julianne pulled up a chair and sat behind him, her eyes fastened on the screen.

He fast-forwarded through videos of seagulls landing on his deck, the wind swaying tree branches, a homeless fellow with a metal detector on the beach. Finally, he slowed when he saw a man walking up the steps to his home. The man wore a baseball cap low over his eyes and a large sweatshirt. Still, something about him seemed familiar....

Julianne gasped. "Is that...?"

Bradley leaned closer. "It could be, but we can't know for sure."

Her hand covered her mouth and she shook her head in disbelief. "I mean, I thought he was alive. But seeing that video...I just can't believe it. He's the same height. He has the same walk."

Bradley watched as the man unlocked the front

door. Where had he gotten the keys? It didn't matter. The man was resourceful.

Now that he was closer to the camera, Bradley got a better look at him. The man definitely resembled Darrell. He was a little heavier. There were more lines on his face. That could happen while living on the run. It hardened a person; it aged them.

Based on the man's purposeful and methodical movements, he'd had all of this planned. He knew how the hurricane shades worked, how to get into Bradley's home, how to work the heater so that the maximum amount of gas would pour into the home.

The time on the video showed that he'd arrived as soon as they left. He'd obviously had the private detective trailing them to insure he had time to do everything he'd wanted. He'd sealed off the house, giving the lethal gas plenty of time to fill the space before they arrived back home. An investigation by detectives had shown that the vents leading to Julianne's apartment had been closed. He hadn't wanted to harm her, just Bradley.

Was it because he cared about Julianne? He probably thought he did, in his own way. But abusers mostly wanted control over their victims and taking away everyone else in Julianne's life would allow him to have just that.

Bradley was determined to not let that happen.

* * *

Julianne couldn't ignore the chills that swept over her as she watched the video feed. Seeing Darrell there made her soul ache with fear.

The man had some kind of morbid plan that involved her. But what? Exactly what was he planning? To kill everyone in her life so she'd have no choice but to run back to him? That would never happen. Besides, how could she run back to him if he was in hiding? What exactly was he hiding from, and why had he faked his death?

She pinched the skin between her eyes, feeling a headache coming on. "I'm at a loss, Bradley. I don't know how to catch Darrell or how to hide from him. I feel like I'm just at his disposal, that whenever he wants to terrorize me and turn my life upside down, he can."

Bradley grabbed her hand and squeezed it. "We're going to get through this."

Julianne found tremendous comfort in hearing the "we" part of his statement. Bradley had been such a support to her. She wasn't sure what she would have done without him.

"Let's talk this through. Right now, we suspect that Darrell killed your therapist and your boss. He killed my secretary and he may have even killed my fiancée." Bradley's voice sounded even and soothing—two things she needed at the moment.

Hearing him say the words aloud only deepened

the ache inside her. What an awful realization for Bradley to have—and a beyond-awful thing for Darrell to do, for that matter. She ran her hands across her face, trying to focus her thoughts. "Why is he targeting both of us? That's what doesn't make sense."

His gaze flickered up to hers. "You've got the degree in counseling. Any guesses?"

She shrugged and heaved in a deep breath. *Focus, Julianne. Focus.* Try to be objective, to look at this like someone on the outside. "He has an obsessive personality. I know he really thought a lot of you. He was always talking about how much he looked up to you. Maybe we're both people that Darrell obsessed over and wanted to control? Your fiancée may have taken time away from your work. She may have shifted your focus, which could have bothered him. And now he's having a hard time letting go of both of us. He still wants to call the shots."

He nodded slowly, his gaze focused in the distance. "You could be onto something. But what about the Mexican drug cartel? How are they involved? That's what doesn't make any sense. They were definitely targeting you, and I want to know why."

She leaned into her chair, her thoughts swirling about in her head. "I have no idea. As far as I know, I've never had any contact with any of the Amigos.

My life was pretty limited when I lived up in the D.C. area. It's not like I had a lot of associations. I mostly had my church and my work, neither of which involved any drug cartels. At least, not that I know of."

"How about when you lived in Norfolk and worked with the inner-city kids? Did Darrell ever go to work with you? Did you see him talking to any of the parents?"

"There weren't very many Hispanics in the program. Just one that I can remember, now that you mention it. And the director. He was Hispanic. But he would never, ever be involved with the Amigos."

Bradley straightened, his curiosity obvious. "Did Darrell ever meet him?"

"Darrell did come to work with me a few times. At the time, I thought he was trying to be sweet, but now that I have a different perspective, I realize it was just to have control over me. When I think back to how he acted that day, I know he was trying to scope out my workplace to see if there were any people there that he should feel threatened by."

"And were there any?"

"I did see him talking to Paul, the director. Paul's parents came here as migrant workers when he was just a toddler. He got his citizenship and has done some really great things for the kids in the area."

"Have you talked to Paul since you moved?"

She shook her head. "No, I haven't. Now that you

mention it, I was kind of surprised he didn't try to keep in touch. But around the time Darrell died, he'd gotten engaged and resigned from his position with the program. Who knows where he is now? He's probably married with a baby on the way."

Bradley swiveled in the chair until he faced his computer. "Let's look him up. See if he's still around."

The implications of what he was saying washed over her. "You really think Paul has something to do with this?"

"We won't know until we talk to him. Maybe he knows something—anything—that could help us find some answers. Right now, we need to figure out what the link is between Darrell and the Amigos. Considering everything that's happened, any lead is a good lead."

Julianne nodded. Were they closer to finding answers? She prayed they were.

THIRTEEN

Two hours later, Bradley and Julianne headed down the road toward a restaurant in downtown Norfolk. Paul still lived in the area, and a simple internet search had turned up his name and phone number. He'd sounded pleasantly surprised to hear from Julianne, but hesitated to meet them. A simple "please" from Julianne had seemed to convince him, although he did mutter, "I have a family now."

Julianne had told him that her life was on the line. That's when he'd said yes.

Bradley and Julianne pulled up to an Irish restaurant located not far from the Elizabeth River. The inside was dark, but it only took a moment for Julianne to find the man sitting at a corner booth with a fizzy soda in front of him and a basket of mozzarella sticks. The way his gaze flittered from side to side made it obvious the man was nervous. But why? That's what Bradley hoped to find out.

Julianne leaned down to give Paul a quick hug before sliding into the booth across from him.

Bradley introduced himself, wondering exactly what was going through the man's head. What had him so on edge?

A waitress appeared and they ordered sodas also. Paul squirmed, obviously uncomfortable in the booth. He was a slight man with a head full of dark hair and the shadow of a mustache and goatee. His clothes were casual—a T-shirt, jeans and zip-up sweatshirt.

"I didn't think we'd ever see each other again," he muttered to Julianne, a slight Mexican accent to his words.

Julianne flashed that beguiling grin of hers that could make the most uptight person relax. It had worked for Bradley on more than one occasion. "Yes, we lost touch, didn't we? Or is it that you purposely stopped communicating?"

His head swayed from side to side as if it weighed a hundred pounds. "You know I always liked working with you, Julianne. And you were great with the kids. I wished every person I'd hired for our program had your enthusiasm and heart."

She rubbed her lips together, looking more relaxed and in control than Bradley had expected. "So what happened?"

He shrugged, his eyes shifting to something in the distance before meeting hers again. "Nothing happened."

Bradley leaned across the table. "I think we all

know that's not true. Paul, Julianne's life is on the line, and we think it has something to do with Darrell. Anything you can tell us will help."

His gaze continued to shift from side to side. His fingers tapped on the table. He licked his lips. The man was obviously anxious. Once again, Bradley couldn't help wondering why. Just then, the waitress set their drinks on the table.

Julianne leaned across the table, her voice as sweet as her countenance. "Paul, did Darrell say something to you when I brought him to work with me two years ago?"

His wandering gaze finally landed on Julianne. "I'm married, you know. I have a six-month old. I gotta keep them safe."

Julianne ran her hand down the side of her soda, leaving a line in the moisture there. Her gaze never left Paul's, though. "Of course you do. Is talking to us putting you in danger?"

Paul leaned closer. Bradley could see his foot fluttering under the table. Bradley's gaze roamed the restaurant again, but he evidently saw no one that made him suspicious.

"Paul, I really need to know. Someone's trying to kill me and, unless I find some answers, they just might get their wish."

His foot tapping reached a crescendo before he finally spread both of his hands on the table and leaned forward, his voice low. "Look, your friend

Darrell found out that my mother was in the country illegally. She was living with me and if Immigration had found out about it, they would have deported her back to Mexico. He threatened to turn her in."

Julianne's eyebrows furrowed together. "Why would he do that?"

"He needed leverage to hold over me."

"Why would he need leverage?" She shook her head as if hoping her thoughts might fall into place.

"He wanted drugs."

Bradley straightened, some of the pieces suddenly coming together. "Drugs? And how would you help him with that? You didn't do drugs, did you?"

"No, man. I'm not into that stuff. I'm clean. I'm a family man."

Bradley didn't break his gaze with the man. "So how could you help him?"

He set his jaw, his nostrils flaring. "My cousin. I don't talk to the man, but he shows up in my life occasionally. Darrell knew about him, somehow."

More pieces came together. "Was your friend a part of the Amigos, by chance?"

"How'd you know that?" His eyes widened in surprise.

"You'd never believe it if we told you," Julianne muttered. "What I don't understand is how Darrell took drugs. The military does drug testing. How did Darrell get past those? He couldn't have."

Bradley shook his head. "I don't think he took the drugs. He dealt them. There's big money involved there. *Big* money." Bradley turned his attention back to Paul. "Did you introduce him to your cousin?"

"I had no choice. I had to look out for my mom. After that, Darrell left me alone. At least, I think he did. Every once in a while, I thought I saw him watching me. As soon as I thought I saw him, he was gone again. Then we got the news that he died." He folded his arms across his chest. "I've gotta admit it, Julianne, I was happy when I heard the news. Happy not only for myself but for you. I didn't like the way he looked at you. He was *loco*. From the time you met him, I saw your happiness slip away. The life was being drained out of you, and it was Darrell's fault."

Julianne grimaced. "I appreciate that, Paul. You don't have to worry. I'm never going to put myself in that situation again. I had my blinders on."

Paul's cell phone beeped. He pulled it from his pocket, hit a button and then his eyes widened. Anxiety was replaced with panic. "It's a text message from the wife. She says there's a strange car sitting outside of our home." He stood. "I knew I should have never come here." He shook his head, running a hand over his face as his features pulled tight. Then he slammed his fist on the table. "Aw, man. Not my wife. I've tried hard to stay away from this junk."

Bradley raised his hands, trying to get the man to slow down. "You need to call the police."

"I can't! My mom…"

Bradley stood, dropping some cash on the table. "Let us help. I'll send some guys to your place. They'll take your family to a safe house until this passes over."

"Who are your guys?" Paul's hands went to his hips.

"I work for a private security contractor. You'll be safe with us."

"No police?" A touch of hope crept into his voice, as well as his gaze.

Bradley shook his head. "No police."

Finally, Paul nodded. "Okay, then."

Julianne's eyes met Bradley's. He could see the worry in the creases around their edges and in the wrinkles across her forehead. He only prayed things got better and not worse.

An hour later, Julianne and Bradley stood on the dry, crispy lawn in front of a small, one-story house in a rundown Norfolk neighborhood. The car in front of his house had sped away as soon as Bradley's men had shown up, and now Paul and his family were on their way to a place where they'd be safe until this storm passed.

Julianne turned to Bradley, still trying to process her conversation with Paul. How could she not have seen what was going on? Never again, she promised herself. Never again would she put herself in a situation like she had with Darrell. God loved her too much for her to allow herself to be treated poorly or to be associated with manipulators.

Bradley looked just as tense about the way events were playing out. All of his muscles appeared rigid and tight. She especially saw it in the set of his jaw. But, even in his distressed state, his gaze remained unwavering, a testament to his inner strength.

"What now?"

He turned until his blue eyes met hers. She was certain she saw affection in his gaze, and that realization made her heart flutter. It had been a long, long time since her heart did flips like it did at the moment. She needed to squash those feelings and fast.

"I have an idea."

She shoved down her emotions and crossed her arms over her chest. "What's that?"

"Where do Darrell's parents live?"

Darrell's parents? She hadn't thought about them in a long time. "About an hour and a half from here, in Petersburg. Why?"

"Have you talked to them since his death?"

She shook her head. "He was estranged from them, for the most part. I only met them once, and they didn't seem thrilled at the introduction. I saw them at his funeral, and that's it. I haven't seen them since."

"I think we should pay them a visit."

She shielded her eyes from the bright sunlight, trying to get a read on Bradley. She had no idea where he was going with this. "What good would that do?"

Bradley grasped her arms and turned her until the sun was blocked by a nearby tree. Then he stepped into the shade also. She couldn't be sure, but he seemed to step closer in the process. *Squash the emotions, Julianne. Squash the emotions.*

"For a moment, let's consider the idea that Darrell is indeed alive. I want to know if they've seen him or had any contact with him. Somehow, he's getting money. He has a motorcycle. He obviously has a place to sleep at night. Who's helping him? He can't be doing all of this alone."

Who *would* help him? "Maybe he's still selling drugs? Maybe that's how he's getting his money." She shrugged. "Maybe Tommy really is helping him out. I doubt his parents are, though. I just can't believe they would do that."

He nodded toward his car. "Let's see if we can find some answers. They may not be helping him, but they may know someone who is."

Julianne didn't move. She appreciated Bradley's help more than she could express. But she knew the pressure Bradley had on him at the moment to wrap up the project he was working on at Eyes. His projects would save the lives of many—not just her in this current dilemma.

He paused and looked back at her through narrowed eyes, as if he sensed her hesitation.

Her hands went to her hips. "What about your project? Your presentation is coming up soon, and I know it's important to you."

He stepped closer. His hands rested on her shoulders. The action seemed to ground her for a moment. "I won't be doing a presentation if I'm dead. I called a couple of guys back at the office, and they're going to handle a few things for me until I return."

She nodded as resolve settled over her. "Let's go, then."

Bradley helped her into the car, and they started down the road. Julianne's thoughts continually turned over the conversation. Just where was all of this leading? Would Darrell's parents have any answers? How would they react to seeing her again? Bradley looked casual as he drove, but his tight grip on the wheel showed how heightened this situation was. He glanced at Julianne. "Tell me about Darrell's upbringing."

Julianne sucked in a deep breath. His upbringing? What was there to tell? "Middle-class family. His dad worked at a factory and his mom was a teacher."

"I know he had at least one brother."

"One and only. Donald. He's a year younger. Last I heard, he wasn't married and he worked as an accountant. They weren't close. They were opposites, as a matter of fact."

"Tragic that he died so close to Darrell."

Julianne tilted her head toward Bradley as she tried to make sense of his words. "What are you talking about?"

"He died about a month before Darrell. I still remember that he had to take leave for the funeral." Bradley's words sounded even and sure.

Julianne shook her head as she tried to merge what she knew with Bradley's revelation. "He didn't die."

"It was a car crash. You didn't know?"

She shook her head again. His words settled over her. Dead? She would have known if that were the case, wouldn't she…?

"Why was Darrell estranged from his family?"

She sucked in a deep breath, trying to gather her thoughts. "All he told me was that his family didn't 'get' him. As soon as he was old enough to leave home, he joined the military. He had limited contact with them afterward."

"Did he say anything about why his family didn't accept him? Any specific reasons?"

"He said he was destined for bigger things than living in a rinky-dink town and working at a factory. I think he got bored easily and got into trouble—not big trouble, but enough that his family worried." She pursed her lips together. "Looking back, I think he probably had some kind of oppositional defiance disorder. He didn't like taking instruction. I think he covered it up pretty well in front of other people, though. He was very intelligent. Too smart for his own good, probably."

"He had a problem with authority and he was obsessive. Not a good combination."

"Not good at all." He had all the right traits that he could either do great things, or terrible things. Had he chosen the terrible? Julianne didn't have to ponder the answer. Yes, he had. Her scar reminded her of that daily.

"He passed the evaluations for the military."

"I think it goes back to his intelligence. I think he's a master at fooling people. He certainly had *me* fooled." She shook her head. "You know, I think something cracked in him after he served in the Middle East. I think he'd always had a bit of an edge to him, but when he got back from Iraq, his eyes seemed vacant. He never talked about it."

"War can do that to a person. There are things

you see over there that you never want to talk about, to think about."

"I can imagine, even though I don't want to imagine any of it. I don't know how you guys did it. But I appreciate the sacrifice. Deeply appreciate it."

He glanced at her again and offered a small smile. "And I deeply appreciate the thank-you."

Silence fell for a few minutes as the tree-lined highway blurred past them. A steady flow of traffic surrounded them and the sun was deceitfully bright for the brisk day.

From out of the quiet, Julianne asked, "Why'd you end up getting out?"

"I'd seen too much death, to be honest. It starts to get to a person after a while. I really wanted to finish what my uncle started, too. The timing was just right."

"It's really admirable what you do, Bradley. I think I had you all wrong."

He glanced at her. "Who did you think I was, Julianne?"

She shrugged. "It's not important."

"You can tell me, you know." He sensed her anxiety and wanted her to relax, wanted her to know that she could tell him anything.

She shrugged again. "I thought you were cold and uncaring."

His voice seemed to catch even before he said the words. "And now you don't?"

Her cheeks turned red, but she didn't back down. "No, I don't. Elle was right."

"What did Elle say?"

"That first night I was here, when she brought me clothes, she said that you were one of the nicest people I'd ever meet. Most people would have run far from this situation by now. At the very least, they would have called the police to come and cart me away." Glancing up at him from beneath her lashes, she smiled at him shyly. "You did neither of those things, and I don't want you to think it's gone unnoticed or unappreciated."

"I think you're awfully brave also, Julianne."

She shook her head. "I don't feel brave. I feel like I've been a coward. I feel like I've let Darrell win."

"The important part is that you pulled yourself together. You're fighting for what you believe in. There's an old saying… Courage isn't found in not fearing something. It's found in facing your fears. That's what you're doing. You don't have to be here right now, Julianne. You could have run away, but you didn't."

She wished she felt as courageous as Bradley seemed to think.

Unfortunately, she felt anything but.

* * *

Bradley felt surprisingly pleased with the exchange he and Julianne had shared during the car ride. He felt as if he'd known her much longer than he had. Their conversation came easily, and Julianne seemed so sweetly sincere. He found it hard to believe that he'd been filled with so much doubt when they'd first met. All of that had dissipated now.

They reached Petersburg, and Julianne told him how to get to Darrell's parents' house. A moment later, they pulled into the neighborhood and stopped in front of a brick ranch. Wood covered the windows and the yard looked as if it hadn't been touched in weeks.

Julianne stared at the destruction from the window of the car. "Wow. What's happened?"

Bradley's jaw was set in a tight lock as he shook his head. "Let's go talk to some of the neighbors and find out."

They climbed from the car and ambled up the steps to the house next door. An older man with white hair and a shaggy mustache opened the door. "Can I help you? Not looking to buy anything, and I don't want any religious tracts."

"We're not selling anything, sir." Julianne put her hands in her pockets. She was the type of person who put people at ease, and Bradley hoped that would work to their advantage now. "We're sorry to disturb you, but we're wondering about the couple that lived next door."

"Terrible tragedy." He shook his head, clucking his tongue as he did so.

"Tragedy?" Bradley tilted his head. He had a feeling that the black hole they were staring out was just getting deeper by the moment.

The man leaned against the door frame, suddenly looking eager to share. "First, their youngest son died in an auto accident. Not even a month later, their oldest boy was killed during a training exercise with the military."

Julianne blanched, her hands coming out of her pockets and resting on her hips instead. "Are you sure their youngest son died first?"

The man kicked a pinecone from the stoop while nodding. "Positive. We went to the funeral."

Bradley saw the confusion across Julianne's face. He rested his hand on her back, trying to steady her. "How about the parents, sir? Where are they now?"

"Died seven, eight months ago. Carbon-monoxide leak."

Alarms went off in Bradley's head, and he tensed as details of the story began to intertwine in his head. "What happened?"

"Space heater. Apparently they went to bed one night and never woke up."

Julianne cleared her throat. "So…it was an accident?"

"'Course it was an accident. Why would someone fill their house with carbon monoxide on purpose? They were two grieving parents. Honestly, they were in so much mourning that I doubt they noticed much. Doubt they even thought about their carbon-monoxide detector." He clucked his tongue. "In the months after their sons died, they stopped cutting their grass and picking up their newspaper. I think their pain swallowed them whole. Doesn't surprise me at all that they didn't notice the space heater like they should have."

"And the house has been vacant since then?" Bradley asked.

"Condemned. Who knows what will happen with it now? Sad, sad story. Makes me glad for the happy years I've lived."

Julianne uncrossed her arms. "Thanks for your help, sir. We appreciate it."

"Why are you asking?" He leaned against the door again, obviously curious for more gossip and information.

Julianne looked up at him. "We're just trying to find some answers. We'd hoped the Lewis's might provide them."

He shook his head solemnly. "Only if they can speak from the grave."

Their deaths did give them some answers, unfortunately.

Bradley led Julianne back to his car. At least they had an idea now of where they needed to look to find the truth.

Julianne blinked back her confusion as she sat in the passenger seat of the car. She kept shaking her head, caught up in a mental conversation with herself as she stared out the front window.

"What are you thinking?" Bradley asked.

"Why wouldn't Darrell tell me that his brother died? We would have been engaged then. I would have gone to the funeral."

"I remember Darrell taking a couple days of family leave for a funeral. It wasn't that much time before Darrell died. What did the neighbor say? A month? That's probably right."

Julianne grabbed Bradley's arm, the urgency of the situation bearing down on her. "Bradley, you've got to find out when his leave started and when exactly his brother died."

"You think he killed his brother, Julianne?" Bradley's voice held a no-nonsense tone, one that chilled her to the bone. Hearing him say the words aloud made everything seem too real, too scary and awful.

She nodded. "I think he killed his family. I just don't know why."

"We might have a lead as to where Darrell is getting all of his money. From drugs—or from life insurance policies."

Julianne shook her head. "But a dead man can't get money from a life insurance policy."

"No, but a dead man who's as smart as Darrell might think of a way to get his hands on it. We've got to do some research."

He started the engine and started down the road. At least they had a place to go from here, Julianne thought. But the heartache of what Darrell may have done to his family gripped her. What kind of monster did something like that? Was he truly capable of being that heartless?

She wrapped her arms over her chest, wishing she could find even a touch of comfort. But right now, not even Bradley's presence offered her reassurance.

FOURTEEN

Bradley pulled over at a rest area and began making phone calls. It took two hours and several phone calls, but he finally verified that Darrell's brother had died two days *after* Darrell requested his leave to attend his funeral. That meant that Darrell had requested time off for the funeral *before* his brother died.

He relayed the information to Julianne. Her face paled and she shook her head. "He's a monster. A horrifically clever monster."

He couldn't argue with her.

A somber silence fell over them as they drove back to Eyes. They didn't have to talk to know what the other one was thinking. They were both letting the information sink in and realizing just the kind of person they were dealing with.

Had Darrell exhibited psychopathic tendencies before he became a SEAL? Had serving in Iraq triggered something in him? There had been other cases—many other cases—of Post Traumatic

Stress Disorder. Bradley knew of Navy SEALs who'd woken up in the middle of the night trying to strangle their wives. Others had become paralyzed with memories and refused to leave their homes. Was what Darrell had seen in Iraq enough to make him kill his family? To kill Vanessa? To try and kill Bradley?

At one time, Bradley would have said no. Now he felt confident that the answer was yes.

Julianne's eyes closed in the seat beside him. Her breathing evened. She'd handled herself like a trooper today. Her analysis of Darrell's personality was dead on. Her questioning of the neighbor had been unwavering. The woman continued to impress him. The whole situation had seemed to open up a fire in her and push her to believe in herself more.

He had to admit that he was totally taken by her. He couldn't stop thinking about her. He caught himself watching her at the most random of times. The thought of anything happening to her unleashed something fierce inside him.

Two weeks ago, he would have said he had no chance at falling in love again. He'd thought what he had with Vanessa was a once-in-a-lifetime thing. But that day Julianne had shown up on the doorstep at Eyes had changed everything.

He believed in God's timing and plan and purpose. He knew that God had a hand in the events of the past week also. Could Julianne see that, though?

They pulled up to Eyes. Bradley had seen no evidence of anyone following them. There'd been no car chases or bullets flying or danger of any other kind. Why did that realization make him suspicious? What was Darrell planning now?

He turned the car off and turned toward Julianne. She stirred, blinking several times as her surroundings came into focus. Then she saw him and smiled.

"There I go sleeping again. There's something about being with you…"

"That makes you fall asleep?"

She yawned, her eyes still hazy from slumber. "That makes me feel safe enough to sleep. To really sleep. I haven't had that in a long time." She looked down shyly before glancing back up. "Thank you."

He took a chance and cupped her cheek. With his thumb, he stroked her soft, silky skin. Her eyes fluttered but she didn't pull away. "I'm glad you feel safe with me."

"Me, too." Her words were almost a whisper. She reached up and her hand covered his. His heart soared with hope. Was there a chance of the two of them having a future together?

"Bradley, I really just want to let you know—"

A quick rapping cut into their conversation.

Bradley turned and scowled when he saw one of the guards standing there at his window. What was Julianne going to say? Would she ever finish that sentence?

"Phone call, sir. The Defense Department."

He dropped his hand, sending an apologetic smile. "Finish this conversation later?"

She nodded, a soft grin that seemed impossible to read across her face. "Later."

The next morning, Julianne met Bradley downstairs for breakfast in the cafeteria. Her cheeks flushed as she remembered their conversation in the car. He'd almost kissed her again. And she'd almost let him.

Thank goodness they'd been interrupted.

But if she were thankful that the kiss didn't happen, why did she keep thinking about the moments beforehand? Why did she keep wondering what it would be like to have Bradley by her side…forever? She didn't want another man in her life trying to control her. But something about Bradley seemed different.

Even having him beside her as they stood in line for breakfast made her feel flustered. He was the kind of man women dreamed about, and not just because of his broad chest, rocklike muscles and towering frame. No, beneath all of that, the man was solid. He was grounded and steady and confident, yet he still had compassion and kindness.

She grabbed a tray, but Bradley pointed to a stack

of disposable containers instead. "Would you mind getting your breakfast to go? I need to go somewhere, and I'd like it if you came with me."

She grabbed a banana and a muffin. "Sure thing. Where are we headed this time?"

"Two places, actually. I'm meeting with someone from the FBI's fraud unit about Darrell's possible insurance scam. I also got a call from someone I know with the DEA." Bradley put a bagel into his container. "He's got someone who's willing to talk to me, someone who used to be with the Amigos. He's going into Witness Protection in return for his testimony."

Her eyes lit up. "You think he'll have some answers?"

"I'm hoping." He glanced her way as he handed a card to the woman at the register.

She wanted to solve this mystery more than anyone. Whatever she could do to get answers, to put Darrell behind bars, she was willing to do.

"Let's go, then."

They grabbed their to-go boxes and some coffee and went out to his car. Julianne was grateful for the coffee that warmed her hands as a cool wind swept over the grounds. Her winter coat wasn't a match for the brisk breeze that continued to whip around them. The conversation was light during the drive—just general chitchat to pass the time. But their attempts at acting normal failed because

Julianne couldn't stop thinking about the events at hand.

Finally, they pulled up to the Norfolk FBI field office. A few minutes later, they were sitting in a conference room with Agent Darden, a man who got right down to business. He pulled up a video on his computer. A grainy bank feed came onto the screen. Agent Darden pointed to a man at the teller counter.

"This is the man who cashed out Donald Lewis's life insurance policy. He disappeared afterward, and we weren't ever able to trace him."

Julianne squinted at the screen. The man wore a ball cap and an oversize sweatshirt. Was it Darrell? Really, it could be anyone. Even with the video being enhanced, it was nearly impossible to make out the man's features.

The agent hit a few buttons and a new feed appeared on the screen. "And here's the video from when Darrell's policy was cashed," the agent said. The same man appeared on screen.

Bradley's jaw clenched. "Who was Darrell's policy left to?"

"His brother. The man in the feed had the proper identification—driver's license, bank account, etc."

"But Donald died before Darrell did." Julianne said it for her own benefit just as much as anyone else's.

"It can take some time for everything to go

through the system. Darrell died only a month after his brother. This man showed up with Donald's driver's license."

Darrell and his brother looked enough alike that they could probably pass for each other. So Donald died, and Darrell cashed the check.

Bradley turned toward the agent. "How about the parents? What about their policy?"

"It was left to the boys but when they both died the check went to an uncle. He never got the check, he said. It must have been intercepted in the mail."

"Where did this uncle live?" Bradley's eyes narrowed with focus. "Locally?"

Special Agent Darden nodded. "Not far from the parents."

So if Darrell were still in the area, he could have gotten it from the mailbox. Some insurance agencies still mailed checks, while others directly deposited them or even hand delivered them.

Bradley rubbed his hands together, shifting his jaw as if in deep thought. "Could we see that video?"

Agent Darden pulled it up with a few clicks on the computer. A man appeared on the screen wearing the same basic outfit—a baseball cap and sweatshirt. Was it Darrell? She couldn't be sure.

She looked more closely and clutched Bradley's arm. "Look, do you recognize that watch?"

"It's a Luxor, isn't it?" Bradley's pressed his lips into a tight line.

Julianne nodded. "Tommy Sanders."

As Bradley filled Agent Darden in on Tommy, Julianne's cell phone beeped. She recognized the number as Becca, another counselor who worked for the hotline. Why would Becca be calling?

She stepped away from the conversation around her and answered. "Hey, Becca. What's going on?"

"Julianne, I need to get right to the point. There are a couple of things I wanted to talk to you about. The first thing is about John." Becca's normally abrasive voice softened. "I heard you found his body."

Julianne shuddered as she remembered that day. "I did."

"The police announced today that the medical examiner's results are in. Someone forced some kind of acid down his throat."

Acid? Her blood ran cold. "That's terrible."

"I know. Isn't it? I hate to think about that happening to him. To anyone, for that matter."

"You said there was something else you wanted to mention?"

Becca sighed. "Yeah, this one concerns you. You know that man who keeps calling and asking specifically to speak with you?"

"Of course. How could I forget?"

"Well, he showed up at the office yesterday demanding to see you."

Julianne shivered. "What happened?"

"He's got some mental problems, for sure. We had to call the police to send him away. He looked crazy."

"Becca, what did he look like exactly?"

"I don't know. About six feet, sandy-blond hair, medium build."

Anxiety cinched her chest muscles. Just like Darrell. Had she been confused this whole time? Did she think her dead fiancé was stalking her when it was really some lunatic she'd counseled on the hotline? If so, how would he have found out so many details about Darrell?

She shook her head, even more confused than before.

After they left the FBI field office, they wound through the streets of Virginia Beach, headed into Norfolk and finally pulled to a stop in front of an ordinary-looking house in an ordinary-looking neighborhood. Bradley rapped on the door and a moment later a man in a suit, introduced as Agent Thomas, ushered them inside.

A Hispanic man sat on a couch, poised tighter than a tiger ready to spring. When Bradley and Julianne walked into the room, he remained motionless except for his eyes, which followed their every movement. The man had a rough edge to him with a scar across his cheek and an air of hostility surrounding him.

Bradley sat across from him, and Julianne decided to stand at the wall. Interrogating people wasn't her specialty. She'd leave that to Bradley and would instead try to be merely an observer.

Bradley leaned forward, a calm demeanor about him. Yet beneath the easygoing persona was an unwavering firmness and strength that showed he was completely in control. "Carlos, thank you for agreeing to meet with us. We need your help."

"Doesn't everybody?" Carlos scowled, his gaze flickering back to Agent Thomas.

"Do you have any idea why the Amigos would target Julianne?" Bradley nodded in her direction.

Carlos glanced back at Julianne again and shrugged. "I have no idea."

"How about guesses? Do you have any of those?"

He shrugged again, apathy staining his gaze. "No."

Bradley shifted and drew in a deep breath that filled his chest and made him seem even more imposing. "Does the name Darrell Lewis mean anything to you?"

The man's eyes sparked in recognition. Still, he shrugged nonchalantly. "Maybe."

"What do you know about him?" Bradley's gaze locked on to his.

"I know Darrell bought drugs from the Amigos using counterfeit funds. I know he was on our most wanted list for a long time. Then he died."

Julianne inhaled sharply. Motive. That was his motive. He faked his death in order to get the cartel off his trail. But they'd found him again. How? And why had he risked showing himself again when he knew it could mean his life?

The truth lingered at the back of her mind. As a counselor, she was well aware of what it meant for someone to have an obsessive personality disorder. Darrell's desire to stay "dead" had been trumped by his desire to make good on his threats to Julianne. Her face went pale at the thought.

Bradley rubbed his chin a moment. "Have you seen him recently?"

The man tensed, his neck muscles stretching taut. "There was rumor that he was alive and in this area. He made our leader, Alexandro, very upset. No one gets one over on him. There's revenge to pay if you try."

Certainly Carlos's words were aimed at himself as much as they were Darrell. If the Amigos were to find Carlos, they'd kill him also.

Bradley straightened, appearing ready to wrap up this meeting. "Last question, Carlos. Any idea why one of the Amigos might try to snatch Darrell's fiancée?"

One shoulder shrugged, and he pulled his head to the side as if squeezing something to his ear. "My guess would be for leverage. Maybe he'd come out of hiding for her."

Cold chills spread over her. So she was a pawn in a deadly game, it appeared. Which side would win? Agent Thomas stood. "We're moving him to another location now. You done?"

Bradley nodded. "I think we got everything we needed. Thanks for letting me come out."

"It's the least I can do for someone who's had my back on more than one occasion. I hope you got something out of this."

"I did. Thank you," he said.

Some of the pieces finally began fitting together in Bradley's mind. At least now he knew how the Amigos and Darrell were connected. Bradley would guess that Darrell got in over his head with drugs and the Amigos. He had no way out except to fake his death. But then the Amigos had found out he wasn't dead, and all they'd wanted was revenge.

And Julianne's life was in danger if the Amigos wanted to use her as leverage, as Carlos had suggested.

Julianne looked pale beside him in the car as they sat outside of the safe house. He put his hand on her neck and gently massaged her knotted muscles there. "What are you thinking?"

"I'm wondering how my life went from normal to crazy in such a short amount of time. My dead fiancé is alive, a drug cartel is terrorizing me and I'm virtually on the run. Where does this leave me?"

"We'll find the answers, Julianne. Just give it some time." He shifted. "Agent Darden mentioned they might exhume Darrell's body. I wasn't sure how you would feel about that."

"I'd love to have some answers. If exhuming his body will give us some, then I'm all for it."

"It might take a couple of days to get through all of the red tape and to get DNA test results back. But at least we'd know."

She looked up at him with those eyes that always melted his heart. "Did Darrell know that when he came back into my life his appearance would lead me here to you? Because you're just as much a target as I am."

"He must have realized you would find me. I would be one of the only people who'd have answers for you. I think he wanted to get me also and that's why he sent that letter and said it was from Dawn Turner."

"He's doing a good job." She shivered and rubbed her arms. "I knew he was messed up, but I had no idea he was *this* messed up. He's…a killer. And he's involved with people who are even worse killers. This just seems surreal."

Bradley hated to admit it but he was beginning to wonder if Darrell was indeed alive. He'd been convinced that someone else was behind all of these incidents when Julianne first showed up. But now all the evidence seemed to be pointing to her fiancé.

FIFTEEN

Bradley had a critical meeting with the engineers designing his new equipment. Julianne insisted that he go and not worry about her. She promised to stay put at the Eyes headquarters, and Bradley assigned a guard to be with her, just in case.

She stayed in her room, on the couch, enjoying some quiet time of reflection. Maybe enjoying wasn't the right word, but it felt good for a moment to feel safe, to have a moment to say some prayers and try to sort out all of her chaotic thoughts.

What if Darrell wasn't alive? What if someone was bent on pulling her into the middle of things? Why would they do that? Why would they kill Darrell's family?

Perhaps Darrell had made someone mad—mad enough that they'd hurt his family. But why show up now and impersonate him?

She tapped her nails on the arm of the couch, trying for the umpteenth time to make sense of things.

Did they think that Julianne had something of Darrell's that they wanted? She had very few of his things when he passed away. She'd had the engagement ring, which she'd flung into the river after his funeral. She had a few cards he'd sent her. She'd burned them. Other than that, she didn't have anything of Darrell's.

But what if someone thought she did? What if he'd left the names of all the drug lords he'd encountered? What if he still had a stash of drugs he'd tried to sell? What if he was trying to obtain U.S. secrets for the other side?

What had happened to all of his stuff? It had probably gone to his family. She'd lost contact with them after the funeral. She disappeared, not wanting to be in contact with them. She couldn't mourn with them the way they needed, so she thought it was easier to just vanish from their lives. Little did she know about the nightmare they faced. Were they aware of how dangerous their son was?

And how did Tommy Sanders fit into all of this? Was he the man pretending to be her stalker? After all, since she'd never seen the man's face—and had only talked to him on the hotline—he could be virtually anyone. But based on Becca's description of the man, he wasn't Tommy.

She rubbed her temples. All of this confusion was giving her a headache.

Tommy Sanders was involved in all of this some-how. She wasn't sure of the details yet, but she knew he was guilty.

Out of curiosity, she put in a call to the firehouse where he was stationed.

An unfamiliar voice answered. "I'm trying to reach Tommy Sanders."

"You're not the only one." The man mumbled something. "I haven't seen him in two days."

"Two days?" That was when she and Bradley had stopped by.

"That's right. He left work early and we haven't seen or heard from him since."

The feeling of dread in Julianne's stomach deep-ened.

The next morning, Julianne filed some papers while Bradley worked in his office. He hadn't got-ten back to the Eyes headquarters until well into the evening. He'd checked in with Julianne, but he looked weary. They'd briefly updated each other before calling it a night.

The phone on the desk rang. It was Detective Spencer.

"Ms. Grace, we were wondering if you and Mr. Stone would come down to the station."

"Is everything okay?"

Bradley appeared behind her, his radar always

on target for whenever bad news might be delivered. Julianne hit the speaker button so he could hear what the detective had to say.

"Last night, there was a house fire down the road from where Mr. Stone lives. One of the smaller rental properties. No one was supposed to be staying there, but apparently there was a squatter. Fire officials found the body after the fire was extinguished."

Bradley stepped closer, his eyebrows furrowed. "This is Bradley, Detective Spencer. What does this have to do with me?"

"Mr. Stone, the face and hands of the man we found inside were burned beyond recognition. But the cell phone we found on the premises had Ms. Grace's number programmed into it."

Trepidation settled between Julianne's shoulder blades. Would this be an answer? Or would this just lead to more questions?

"We'll be right there," Bradley said.

As soon as they hung up, Julianne looked back at Bradley. "Do you think it's Darrell?"

He shook his head. "I don't know. Maybe the detective can shine some light on it. Whoever the man was, he had some connection to you."

Twenty minutes later, they reached the police station and were escorted to Detective Spencer's office. "Thanks for coming."

"What can you tell us, Detective?" Bradley asked.

He raised his eyebrows in a manner that showed he had something big to share. "Have a seat first. Believe me, you'll want to be sitting down for this."

They lowered themselves into the chairs across from his desk. Julianne fidgeted as she anticipated what he might say. Would this nightmare finally be over?

Detective Spencer clasped his hands together and stared at them for a moment. "I told you about the fire. What I didn't tell you about were these." The detective scattered something across the table.

Julianne gasped when she saw pictures of her and Bradley there. Her and Bradley eating at the seafood restaurant. Standing on Bradley's deck. Walking into the police station.

She glanced up at Bradley, unable to conceal how startled she was. "He was watching us every step of the way."

Bradley moved a couple more pictures out of the way. There were more photos. Pictures of her meeting with her counselor, Alan. Pictures of her walking into staff meetings with her boss. Pictures of her at church.

A tremble started at her core and spread to her limbs. "Do you have a description of the man who died in the fire?"

"Only the preliminary findings. Six feet tall. Probably in his early thirties. White. Male."

Julianne glanced at Bradley. "That fits Darrell's description."

Bradley turned back to the detective, hard lines appearing at the corners of his eyes and wrinkling his forehead. "How'd the fire start?"

"It's not clear yet, but right now it looks like it started outside the home."

"What if the Amigos found Darrell and started that fire?" Julianne asked Bradley.

"It's a possibility," Bradley agreed. He filled the detective in on everything they'd found out.

"There's something else we need to address with you, Ms. Grace." The detective's piercing eyes bore into hers.

She shoved down the discomfort she felt under his stare. "What's that?"

He shoved a piece of paper forward. "We found this note with the pictures."

She looked down at the plain piece of white paper with words scribbled across it.

Meet me at 1210 Ginger Court at 11:00 a.m.
Love, Julianne.

Her eyes widened. "I never sent this. That's not even my handwriting."

The detective's expression hardened. "I'm beginning to question your involvement in all of this, Ms. Grace."

She shook her head, panic beginning to rise. "I'm being set up. I never sent that note."

"There's one more thing I needed to mention to you, Ms. Grace." The detective continued to stare at her.

Exactly where was he going with this line of questioning?

She shifted, her breaths coming in quick spurts. "What's that?"

"We got Diane's home computer and examined it for evidence as to what may have happened to her."

"Okay…"

"We found some correspondence between Bradley's secretary and someone with the initials D.L."

Julianne blinked. "Darrell? Diane was communicating with Darrell?" Sure, they'd found his phone number on her desk. But Julianne assumed that had been just another mind game Darrell was playing, that he'd called and left his number simply as a red herring.

The detective tilted his head in a no-nonsense manner. "The emails mentioned that you were coming down here and getting some information."

"I came here spontaneously. There's no way she could have known I was coming. That's simply impossible." Julianne shook her head so hard she felt as if the room were shaking. She didn't like where this conversation was going.

"Unless you're trying to pull one over on us all."

She glanced back at Bradley. Did he believe her? Or were his doubts greater than his faith in her also?

Two days passed with no updates. Bradley made sure that Julianne was secure at the Eyes headquarters and, because of that, there had been no more attempts on her life. They'd eaten their meals together, she'd helped him in the office and in the evenings they'd hung out with Jack, Rachel, Denton and Elle.

For just a moment, things felt normal. Eerily normal.

But Bradley cherished that time. He liked seeing Julianne smile. He liked seeing her interact with his friends. She had an easygoing personality and a laid-back smile that could put anyone at ease.

But there were also a lot of suspicions circling her. Was she being set up? Or was his earlier theory correct that all the enemy had to do was send in a beautiful woman? He didn't believe that, despite the doubt that nagged at him.

But why would that correspondence be found on Diane's home computer? What possible explanation could there be? And what about the note found at the scene of the house fire?

Even with all of that confusion, he knew he was head over heels in love with her.

He'd realized earlier how deeply attracted he was to her. But the past couple of days, though tension over the events at hand always simmered beneath the surface, had been a nice reprieve from the past week.

In the meantime, they waited for Detective Spencer to call with an update, a confirmation that the man they'd found was Darrell and that maybe this nightmare would finally be behind them. At the very least, hopefully they'd call with an update on Tommy or the insurance fraud or the person behind John's death. Every time the phone rang, they both stared at each other a moment before one of them would answer.

Right now, Julianne tapped on the computer, helping him to type up some paperwork before his big meeting. The phone rang. She cast him that familiar glance. He nodded, and she picked up the line. Her eyes widened, and she motioned for him to come into the front office.

"I'm going to put you on speaker." She hit the button and Detective Spencer's voice came over the line.

"We've got some results that we wanted to share with you. Are you sitting down?"

A shot of adrenaline pumped though his veins. "We're good, Detective. Go ahead."

"We got the autopsy results back. The body we found in the house was not Darrell Lewis."

Julianne's shoulders visibly drooped. Bradley rested a hand there, trying to offer her some small comfort.

"Ms. Grace, does the name Clayton Roberts means anything to you?"

She shook her head. "No, nothing. Why do you ask?"

"He was identified as the man from the fire. He's from northern Virginia."

She tensed under Bradley's hand. "That's where I'm from."

"Police visited his apartment and found more evidence that he's connected to you."

"Can you share what that evidence is?" Bradley shifted, not liking where this was headed.

The detective paused a moment as if gathering his thoughts. "I can say this. The man had a lot of pictures of you. And we found the emails you sent him."

"The emails *I* sent him?" Julianne's voice almost came out as a whisper, each syllable cracking with emotion.

"You might want to consider hiring a lawyer, Ms. Grace."

"But I didn't do anything."

"The evidence is to the contrary." The detective's voice sounded firm, leaving little room for argument.

"Are you going to arrest me?" Fear filled her voice.

"Not yet, but we're collecting evidence."

She closed her eyes, despair biting deep.

Bradley pulled her into his arms, realizing that hopelessness was beginning to overwhelm Julianne as more evidence mounted against her.

The nagging doubts in his mind became stronger, but he pushed them away. No, Julianne wasn't guilty. She couldn't be…could she?

Julianne felt as if the whole world had gone crazy.

Bradley's arm remained at her waist, holding her steady and keeping her from giving in to the weakness that made her knees want to buckle.

"It's going to be okay," Bradley insisted.

She shook her head as thoughts collided inside her mind. "Darrell is setting me up. He has to be. Why else would this be happening? I couldn't have met anyone yesterday. I was here at Eyes. You had a guard outside of my room."

"The police will realize that." His voice sounded firm and steady, but had just a touch of doubt began to creep in? She couldn't blame him. Someone had done a good job insuring that she looked guilty.

She ran her hands over her face, reality crushing her. Even her breathing felt labored as she considered the evidence against her. "Oh, Bradley. I just don't know what to think sometimes. I don't know how to make sense of all of this. All I know to do is pray."

Just then, Bradley's phone rang. It was Agent Darden. Bradley put it on speaker, and Julianne stepped closer, anxious to hear what he had to say.

"Mr. Stone, Ms. Grace, I wanted to let you know that we got preliminary results on the body. There was a fifty percent DNA match to Darrell Lewis."

Julianne's hand instinctively went to her heart as his words settled over her. "Fifty percent?"

"We're going to run a few more tests, but all of our best guesses are that it's Darrell in that grave. He is indeed dead."

Julianne's heart twisted as Bradley hung up. The news was both a relief and a disappointment. If Darrell wasn't alive and behind everything, then who was?

Bradley frowned beside her. "It looks like Darrell really is dead."

She blanched. "Really? I felt so certain…"

"I was halfway convinced myself, Julianne."

"Does this leave us back at square one?"

Bradley grasped her arms. "Julianne, what did Darrell's brother look like?"

"Donald? He looked too similar to Darrell, I suppose." Realization washed over her. "You think maybe Donald is behind this?"

"It's a possibility."

And at this point, they couldn't leave any stone

unturned. No, Julianne's life depended on it. The total irony was that the perpetrator wasn't *literally* trying to kill her—instead, someone out there was trying to make her miserable and obliterate anything good that came her way.

That evening, Julianne couldn't seem to keep her thoughts focused on anything around her. They continued to go back to another place in time. She sat in the lobby at Eyes, staring at that blazing fireplace that seemed to warm the entire room.

Bradley sat beside her on the couch, and she could feel his eyes on her.

"What are you thinking, Julianne?"

"I just can't believe that Darrell really did die. This whole time I thought that he'd secretly survived somehow. I should have listened to you when you said that could never happen." She shook her head.

Bradley's hand rested on her neck, his fingers gently massaging the kinks away. "I even believed that he might be alive, Julianne. Anyone in your shoes would consider the possibility."

She swallowed, her throat burning as she dared to glance over and meet his gaze. "What about Vanessa? How does her death tie in with all of this? And the Amigos? There are still so many puzzle pieces that don't seem to fit."

"I keep coming back to Tommy. We need to find him. As soon as we do, we'll have some answers."

Tommy. Could he really be the mastermind behind all of this? Or maybe it was Donald? Was he secretly still alive? Why had Diane gotten involved? There were so many questions. "So maybe Tommy killed Darrell's parents and then collected the money? Maybe he was mixed up with the Amigos, as well—maybe Darrell got him involved. Maybe that's how he could afford that watch."

"I have to wonder if he got himself so far into debt that he's trying to get his hands on the plans I'm developing. Enemies of the United States would pay big money for them. Tommy always asked a lot of questions about my uncle's work. Maybe that wasn't a coincidence."

Bradley pulled her closer, and her heart unwillingly soared. Although she'd secretly dreamed of being held in his arms just like this, there was too much uncertainty right now to truly savor the moment. "Maybe the end's finally in sight," he murmured softly into her hair.

She nodded, unsure of what else to say.

He reluctantly stepped back. "What are you going to do when this is over?"

She shrugged. "I don't know." And she didn't. She had no idea, mostly because she didn't really have time to think about anything other than the present.

"You should stay."

His words caused her heart to swell. Had she heard him correctly? Did he mean what she thought he did? She raised her gaze to his, afraid too much truth would show in her eyes. "You think?"

His gaze latched onto hers. "I do."

A million doubts and uncertainties seemed to flutter through her mind, each trying to find a place to land permanently. She shooed them away, searching for an honest response. "I'm not very good with relationships, you know. I always pick the wrong guy."

"Is that what you think about me?"

His eyes just looked so sincere, so earnest and trustworthy. Even with everything she'd been accused of, he was still having this conversation with her. He still believed in her, and that meant the world to her. "No, I think you're perfect. And that scares me. I've got to be able to stand on my own two feet."

He still didn't break his gaze. "But you can't be afraid to rely on other people. That's what life is about. Holding other people up. But not trying to control them."

"You've really showed me that, Bradley. You've never tried to make me fit a mold. I appreciate it."

"I would never make you try to be someone you're not."

She believed him.

But believing in him scared her to death.

She looked at her hands, at the way they were laced together in her lap. She swallowed, her throat burning. "I should go to bed," she croaked out.

"Let me walk you up." He started to stand.

She shook her head. "No, please. I can walk up by myself."

Confusion gleamed in his eyes. "I don't mind."

"Really. I'll be okay. I should…go."

Before he could argue, she hurried up the stairs and into her room. No sooner had she closed the door, did her phone buzz. Had Bradley texted her?

Steal the plans or Bradley dies. D.L.

The blood drained from her face.

D.L.

Donald Lewis?

SIXTEEN

Steal the plans? She couldn't possibly steal the top secret plans that Bradley had developed. She had no clue where they were even. He'd said something about keeping them under lock and key—which probably meant they were at his house—but she hadn't the faintest idea where to start searching.

Would D.L. make good on his threat? If she didn't deliver something to him…would he really kill Bradley?

Meanwhile, she was being set up to look like the culprit in all of this.

The noose seemed to be tightening with each second.

What was she going to do?

She threw her head back into the pillow atop her bed.

Was there a way to win in this situation? It didn't feel like it.

The police thought she did it. Now, if she didn't

get involved then Bradley would die. If she did get involved, Bradley would never trust her again.

Lord, what am I supposed to do?

She closed her eyes.

She had no idea. She had absolutely no idea.

Bradley rolled over in bed, his thoughts pounding at this temple.

Someone was setting Julianne up to look like the bad guy. They wanted to ruin her...but why?

Could Donald Lewis actually be alive and be behind this?

Or was Tommy Sanders involved somehow?

How had Diane gotten tangled up in this mess? Had she been involved before Bradley hired her? Had she wanted the job in order to get an inside track into what was going on here?

There were so many unanswered questions and the clock seemed to be ticking. He didn't know what would happen at the end of this. Would Julianne be arrested? Was someone trying to get their hands on his weapons?

He sighed.

He just didn't know. And he didn't like not knowing. He was the kind of guy who found solutions. He didn't let problems hold him back. Yet, in this case, he didn't know how to find the solutions.

Lord, I've relied on myself too much. Now I'm in

a situation where You're the only one who can help. Please, clear my thoughts. Make the truth evident.

He closed his eyes, scenarios still turning over in his mind.

But any way he looked at it, the ending wasn't happy.

Jack met Bradley in the hallway the next morning when he was on his way to get Julianne for breakfast.

"I got an odd message last night. Someone emailed me and suggested I search the cushions in the apartment below your house."

Bradley stopped. "Who was the email from?"

"Unsigned."

"Julianne's being set up." Anger surged in him at the thought.

"I'd still like to send a couple of guys over to check. Is that okay with you?"

Bradley pulled his lips into a tight line before offering a terse nod. "Of course."

"Just keep your eyes open, Bradley. I like Julianne. I really do. But we have to be careful in this line of work."

"Agreed." They'd see she was innocent. Bradley had no doubt about that.

So why was it that when he knocked on her door five minutes later an unseen weight pressed on his chest? Her eyes fluttered around, hardly meeting his, and the weight pressed harder.

They barely said a word through breakfast. Just as they went up to his office, his cell phone rang. Jack. He sucked in a deep breath and stepped away from Julianne before answering.

This would be good news. It had to be good news.

"I hate to be the one to tell you this, but there were some documents tucked into the couch cushion, Bradley."

"What kind of documents?"

"They weren't exactly your plans and drafts and prototypes, but there was information on your designs. Enough that it would give terrorists an idea of what you were doing. Enough to make the Department of Defense nervous."

"I understand."

"You've got to question her, Bradley. Do you want me to do it?"

His heart twisted until finally he shook his head. "No, I will. But thank you."

He hung up and drew in a deep breath. This was one conversation he didn't want to have. But there was no other choice.

He walked over to Julianne's desk. She looked up, those eyes—deceitfully innocent?—stared back up at him.

"Is everything okay?"

"No, it's not. We got a tip that you had taken some documents from our headquarters, Julianne. I knew it couldn't be true, but we had to send some men to double-check. Sure enough, the documents were there in the couch cushions."

Her eyes widened and she shook her head forcefully. "I didn't leave those there. I'm being set up. I don't have any of your plans. I don't even know where you keep them."

"Can I see your phone?"

Her face went white. "My phone? Why?"

"Because I just need to check your messages. It's the easiest way to prove that what you're saying is true." His face softened. "This isn't just about me and you anymore, Julianne. They've gotten Jack involved, as well as the Department of Defense. I've got to rule out every possibility."

She shook her head, tears glimmering in her eyes. "Sure." She pulled it out of her back pocket and slapped it into his hand.

Her obvious hurt made sorrow clutch at his heart. But he had to check—he had to do what he could— to prove to Jack that she was innocent.

She crossed her arms over her chest and stared in the distance as he pulled up her text messages. There would be nothing there and they'd be able to put all of this behind them. This was just a formality, he rationalized.

He blinked at the message he saw.

Got the plans. Thanks for your help, Julianne.
You're one in a million.

He had left Julianne alone in his house and in his
office. She had been asking a lot of questions about
his projects. Could his initial thoughts have been
correct? Was her appearance here simply a ploy?

All of the events of the past several days flashed
back to him. How in all of those dangerous situations, she'd never once been injured. How the killers always seemed to anticipate their next move.
How easily she could put people at ease and cap-
tivate them.

Was that because Julianne was feeding someone information?

The truth crashed into his heart. He didn't want
to believe it, but the evidence seemed to confirm
his worst fears. Julianne had been playing him this
whole time.

Her face seemed to show sincere confusion. But
he'd fallen for her charms before. She knew how to
fool people, knew how to appear innocent.

"How do you explain this?" He held up her
phone.

Her eyes scanned the message and she shook her
head, looking briefly toward the sky as her eyes
continued to brim with unshed tears. "If I told you
the truth you wouldn't believe me. I'm not a part

of this vast conspiracy, Bradley. How could you think that?"

"I don't know what else to think. I don't want to do this, Julianne, but I think I should take you down to the police station for questioning."

She stared back at him and raised her chin. "Whatever you think is best." Her words were said with a level, even tone that conveyed her hurt.

They stared at each other, all the beautiful trust between them shattering like fragile glass in a windstorm.

A mixture of fury, outrage and grief washed over Julianne. How could Bradley think she'd do something like this? Did he really think that she set all of this up as a means of obtaining his classified plans? His life may have a touch of James Bond and Mission Impossible, but hers certainly didn't. She wasn't a spy embarking on a lethal mission. Silence stretched between them as they cruised down the back roads of Virginia Beach toward the police station. With each turn of the wheel, her brooding became deeper and a hopeless feeling claimed her.

"I'm going to be arrested, aren't I?" she whispered.

"I don't know."

"How could you possibly think that I would do something like that?" Hurt slammed into her chest, and she tried not to blanch.

"I'm the only one who's almost died here. Maybe there's a reason for that."

She willed her voice to remain even, despite her instinct to scream her innocence. She licked her lips, and her voice sounded eerily calm as she said, "If I wanted to take those files and run, I could have done it a million times already. I could be long gone."

His gaze was hard, unrelenting. "Maybe you've already taken some of the documents. That's what the text message seemed to indicate."

"You're being ridiculous." He really thought she might be guilty. How could he? She raised her chin, not backing down. "Can't you see I'm being set up here?"

His jaw flexed, a sure sign that he didn't believe her. "Why would someone set you up?"

Before she could respond, something popped. The car swerved toward the ditch. Bradley righted the vehicle but not before the bumper collided with a tree. The car came to a complete halt.

Bradley glanced at her. "Are you okay?"

"What just happened?" She rubbed her neck, her muscles sore from the impact.

"Gunfire. We've got to get out of here."

Someone appeared beside Julianne's door. She dared to look up at the man standing there with a gun in hand. Her heart stammered in her ears.

Would this be how it all ended?

* * *

"Get out! Now!"

Julianne jerked her head toward the voice. Tommy Sanders stood there, a gun trembling in one hand and blood trickling down his left temple. The man looked as if he hadn't slept in days—his clothes were rumpled, the beginnings of a beard shadowed his face and his eyes looked haggard.

"We're getting out. Just don't hurt Julianne," Bradley muttered. He nodded toward the door, letting her know she should do as Tommy said.

She opened the door and climbed out, a tremble beginning in her hands. Bradley appeared at her side.

"You both need to come with me."

"Where are we going?" Bradley asked.

"I'm the one making demands here, not you," Tommy muttered. "Now go."

Despite Bradley's accusations, he still stepped in front of Julianne, blocking her from the gun's aim. She noticed the action, but resolved not to let it affect her. He hadn't even given her the benefit of the doubt.

"Tommy, what's going on?" Bradley's voice sounded amazingly steady and calm. "Tell us. Maybe we can help you."

Tommy looked behind him, the wariness leaving in his eyes and replaced with...fear? "We don't have much time. They're going to be here any minute."

Bradley remained the picture of composure. "Who's going to be here?"

Tommy waved the gun around again, his hands trembling so badly that Julianne worried he might accidentally fire. "The Amigos. They're on my trail. They have been for a while now."

Julianne stepped forward, tired of hiding behind other people, tired of living in fear. "Why did you set up Clayton Roberts? Why'd you blackmail him, Tommy?"

A knot formed between his eyes and he glanced behind him again before looking back at Julianne. "Who's Clayton Roberts?"

Was he serious? Did he really not know? Or was this just part of his plan? "The man you black-mailed up in northern Virginia." Julianne tried to imitate Bradley and remain calm. It didn't work. Her voice cracked on "Virginia."

Tommy shook his head, looking annoyed on top of frantic and fearful. "I have no idea what you're talking about."

Bradley nudged in front of her again. "What are you doing here now, Tommy?"

His gaze focused on Julianne. "I need her."

"She isn't up for grabs."

"You don't understand. Julianne's the only way I'm going to get the Amigos off my trial. Without her, I'm as a good as dead."

"You're already as good as dead." Bradley backed

up a step closer to her. That still didn't make up for how quickly he'd lost faith in her. She'd almost decided to give a relationship with the man a chance.

Tommy glanced behind him once more. His anxiety only added to Julianne's. Any hope she had of things turning out well was quickly fading.

"We don't have much time. I don't want to hurt anyone."

"You've already hurt a lot of people."

He frowned at her. "I don't know what you're talking about. I haven't hurt anyone. Sure, I've stolen some things, but I've never actually harmed a living soul."

"What about Darrell's parents? We know you cashed out their life insurance policy."

He wiped the sweat from his brow. "I had to. It was part of the terms of the person blackmailing me."

Bradley nudged her behind him again. "Who was blackmailing you?"

"It might sound crazy, but I thought it was Darrell. Whoever it was threatened to reveal all of my indiscretions. And I had a lot of them. Too many women. Too many of the wrong women. I would have been kicked out of the military. I've got to put an end to all of this. It's been going on for too long."

"You're not leaving here with Julianne."

"We'll see about—" Before he could finish his sentence, a shot rang out. Tommy crumpled to the ground.

* * *

Julianne screamed.

Bradley reached for the gun in the holster at his shoulder when four men surged from the woods and surrounded them. "Not so fast, señor."

Reality hit Bradley. The Amigos. They'd found them, and they were outnumbered.

How could he have ever thought that Julianne was a part of this? That note was just another ploy in someone's twisted game. He wished he could turn to her now and apologize, but he couldn't. Was it too late for them—on all fronts?

Julianne clutched his arm from behind. He could feel her fear as she squeezed.

Four men. He recognized one from the restaurant. The one speaking was Alexandro, the gang's leader.

And they wanted Julianne.

Wanted her badly enough that they'd killed Tommy. The man lay on the ground, a pool of blood around him and his chest absent of breath.

Bradley raised his hands in the air, still keenly aware of the gun at his shoulder, within reach but off-limits.

"What do you want?"

Alexandro pointed with his gun to Julianne. "We need her."

"You can't have her."

He stepped closer. "I don't remember giving you an option."

"You'll have to get by me first."

Alexandro sneered. "I don't think that will be a problem."

"Bradley…" Julianne whispered. "Just let me go. Put an end to all of this."

"Over my dead body."

She gasped at his words. But he meant them. He'd sacrifice himself for Julianne if he had to. But she had a better chance of surviving if he were alive than if he were dead.

Alexandro held up his gun to Bradley's face. "I can arrange that."

"Please, I don't want anyone to be hurt. I'll do whatever you want." Julianne tried to slip around him, but Bradley pushed her back.

"I'm not going to let you do that, Julianne." He looked at Alexandro. "Why do you want Julianne?

"We have unfinished business."

"I've never even met you before. What kind of business could we possible have together?" Julianne's voice wavered.

"You ask too many questions. Now come with us, or I'm going to shoot." Alexandro cocked his gun.

"No! Don't shoot. I'll go with you."

"You're not going with them, Julianne. They'll kill you."

"If I stay here, they'll kill *you*." She stepped out. "I'm going with them."

Just as Alexandro reached for her, Bradley shoved him out of the way. Alexandro fell to the ground. There wasn't much time. The other three men closed in. "Run, Julianne!"

She stared at him. "I can't."

"You have to."

The first bullet flew, plunging into a nearby tree. As another one flew, Bradley tackled Julianne to the ground and out of range. He shoved her away. "Go!"

She pulled her gaze from his and nodded. Just as she dragged herself from the ground, another shot fired. It hit Bradley in the chest.

The last thing he remembered was Julianne's scream.

Julianne trembled as the gun was pointed at her temple. Worse than the physical danger was the emotionally devastating realization that Bradley could be dead.

No, he couldn't be. But she didn't have time to check on him. The bullet had hit him in the chest. Was there any way he could have survived that?

A van squealed to a stop only feet away. Alexandro pulled her toward the open door and pushed her inside.

Grief hit her in waves. She'd seen the look in

Bradley's eyes. He cared about her. Despite his ear-lier accusations, he believed her. More than any-thing, she wanted a chance to rectify things. Now that would never happen. Could he see the same thing reflected in her gaze? Had he been able to see how much she cared about him?

The Amigos crowded in and the van squealed off. Where were they taking her? She had to stay focused. She'd grieve for Bradley later. Right now, she needed to stay alive.

She glanced at the men in the front seat. "What are you going to do to me now?"

"You'll find out," Alexandro muttered.

The harshness of his words caused anxiety to clench her stomach.

She knew exactly what they were going to do. They were going to use her as bait to try to lure Darrell out. Then they would kill him. When they finished with him, they'd kill her also, just for kicks.

They bumped along the road. Had any of the neighbors heard the gunshots and called the po-lice? Was there anyone left to help her?

She could see nothing in the back of the work van. There was only the smell of stale cigarette smoke, body odor and fuel. Two men sat up front and the other four in the back with her. Each man had a gun.

"Have you been following me?"

"We're not the only ones," Alexandro sneered.

"Who else?"

"Don't you worry your pretty little head over it, sweetheart."

"Are human lives really worth it?"

Alexandro scowled. "Lives are disposable. No one crosses me. No one."

She shivered again. *Lives are disposable.* Who thought like that?

She knew. Someone who wouldn't give a second thought to killing her.

SEVENTEEN

Bradley opened his eyes and took in his surroundings. The bullet had knocked the wind out of him.

He touched the spot on his chest where it had hit. The area was still tender.

He pulled his shirt back and touched the protective armor he wore underneath. Another new design. He'd decided to test it out today to see if it was as comfortable as it had been designed to be. He'd had no idea he'd be able to test its effectiveness, as well.

He pulled himself to his feet. He had to get to Julianne. He had no time to waste.

A van squealed away in the distance, too far to get a license plate.

He ran to his car and jumped inside. He had to follow them before their lead became too great. He called the cops to report what had happened as they sped down the road.

The car puttered, but finally started. He shoved the gear into Reverse and hit the pedal. The car groaned but, despite the sputtering, traveled backward. Once back on the road, he threw the car in drive and sped after them.

He spotted the van ahead. He kept it in sight until he reached the main highway. In the distance he saw the van pull through an intersection. He wasn't going to make it in time. He slammed his hand on the steering wheel. "Come on, come on."

It was no use. The cars in front of him had stopped. The only way to get around them was to plow down the pedestrians on the sidewalk. The van disappeared from view.

He had to find Julianne. There was no other choice.

The van stopped and, a moment later, Julianne was shoved out. The sun had set and darkness surrounded them. Where were they?

Her gaze scanned the area. The beach? Had they brought her to the beach?

She recognized the area. It wasn't too far from Bradley's house. The parking area was called Little Island and beachgoers flooded the spot in the summer. But what were they doing here?

"Come on, señorita." Alexandro jerked her toward a four-wheeler. "Too bad you don't have a coat."

He pushed her onto the back of the all-terrain

vehicle. "Hold on or get run over," the gang leader warned with a laugh.

She reached for something—anything—to hold on to rather than the man in front of her. Just as the ATV charged forward, her hands connected with the grate behind her. She held on, knowing that the four-wheeler behind her would indeed run her over if she slipped off.

They headed south on the beach road. But it ended soon...

Back Bay, she realized. They were taking her into a wooded beach area restricted to vehicles. Who would find her out here? There were places to hide, places where no one would find her. Of course, they knew that, didn't they? That was part of their plan.

Despair threatened to consume her. She'd held on to a smidgen of hope that there would be a happy ending. With each turn of the wheels, that hope faded. She had no idea how she was going to get out of this one...only by God's grace.

Lord, help me. Help me to trust You more.

She cared about Bradley. She'd known that she cared about him for a while now, but she hadn't wanted to admit it. She couldn't ever remember having a man in her life that had made her feel so loved, protected...and safe. She hadn't felt safe in a long time.

Would she survive long enough to tell him that?

Her fingers curved tighter under the rack behind her as the road became rougher. A frigid wind cut through her sweater and dress pants. She'd already lost feeling in her nose and most of her face.

Thirty minutes into the trip, into the heart of the night and the heart of the unknown, they stopped. Alexandro pulled her from the back of the ATV. Here, not far from the ocean, the wind was even more frigid and cut right through her clothing.

Alexandro shoved her against a tree as the rest of his gang surrounded her.

Fear—true, palpable fear—leaped through her. What would they do to her now? The look in their eyes was anything but merciful. Chills crawled over her skin. Nausea roiled in her gut.

"What do you want with me?" Her voice sounded shaky, and she hated hearing the terror there. But she couldn't conceal it. Every part of her body trembled.

Alexandro pulled a knife out and turned toward the trees. "We've got her. Now come out or she dies."

"How do you know someone followed us here? They would need a four-wheeler to follow us here. We would have heard him."

"He's a resourceful guy, in case you didn't know that." Alexandro ran the knife along her throat, not hard enough to produce blood. But Julianne knew it was there, that its edge could easily claim her life.

She tensed, afraid to move for fear of prodding the knife into herself. "Isn't that right, Darrell?"

"What makes you so sure that this Darrell person still cares about me?"

"Because he could have killed you more than once already and he hasn't."

She found both comfort and fear in his words.

Bradley. Where was Bradley? Maybe he was safe, at least. That was her only comfort.

God ruled the wind and waves. Certainly, he ruled over her life, too. Everything was in his hands.

"Come out, come out wherever you are," Alexandro taunted. He paced in front of her. "I know you don't want anything to happen to your woman here. You have to the count of ten. Then I'm going to start using my knife."

Bradley reached the intersection and his head swerved from side to side. Which way had they gone? Straight, he decided. They'd gone straight. He pushed the accelerator, going as fast as he could.

He reached the road leading to Sandbridge. Could they have gone toward his house? He didn't know. But his gut told him to try it. He had nothing else to go on at the moment.

His heart raced as he sped down the road. He had to get to Julianne in time. He had to.

He slowed as he reached the road that ran alongside the beach. His eyes scanned the area for a sign of the black van. Just then, his cell rang. He glanced at the screen. The detective.

"Anything?" Detective Spencer didn't waste any time with niceties.

Bradley shook his head, slowing considerably as residences came into view. "Not yet. I think they may have come down to the beach. No idea why, though."

"We have guys on the way now. We're sending out a helicopter to see if we can track them through the air."

The need to find Julianne pressed on his shoulders. "We don't have any time to waste, Detective."

Bradley hung up and dropped the phone into the passenger seat. Where had they gone? His eyes scrutinized the homes around him and a few businesses located across the road. He saw nothing out of the ordinary. Just what were they up to?

They could have pulled into a garage, he realized. He shook his head. They wanted to lure Darrell out. Just where did they plan to do that? And what did they plan to do to Julianne in the process?

Anger warmed his blood at the thought and his fingers tightened their hold on the steering wheel.

He reached the end of the road and pulled into a public parking area to turn around. That's when he saw the van. He braked. No one loitered around it. Were they inside?

There was only one way to find out. He pulled to a stop beside the vehicle. Drawing his gun, he exited his car and slowly, carefully approached. There were no signs of movement, indicating that either no one was here or that they didn't want him to think they were.

He peered inside. Empty. Where had they gone?

He stepped back and gathered in his surroundings. The beach. The snack shack. Public restrooms. A tall stretch of condos. Across the street, away from the beach, was an empty field of dune grass, surrounded by a small ocean tributary. Far beyond that was an RV park.

And at the end of the road was…Back Bay. The perfect secluded spot, especially in the winter when it was barely patrolled by rangers even. He knew where he had to look.

Headlights coming down the road grabbed his attention. A golf cart. He jogged toward the driver, waving him down.

"I'll trade you my Mercedes for the golf cart."

The older man raised his eyebrows. "You think I'm a fool?"

"It's a life or death emergency. Please." He dangled his keys in front of him.

"Hope you don't regret it."

"Oh, I won't." He handed the man his keys and jumped in the golf cart. The vehicle was quiet enough that he could approach without anyone hearing him. He cut the headlights and headed toward Back Bay, calling the detective on the way. He'd need back-up. Lots of back-up.

The cart bumped down a dirt path filled with tree roots and divots of sand. He paused and listened. Nothing. Not yet. But they had to have come this way.

He continued down the path, darkness surrounding him. Farther up the trail, he paused. Voices. He definitely heard voices. He left the golf cart and started down the path by foot.

"Come out, come out wherever you are," someone with a distinct Mexican accent called.

Bradley crouched behind a tree. In the distance, the moonlight illuminated a clearing in the trees. He spotted Julianne. Alexandro had a knife to her throat.

Then he saw the blood already running down her jaw.

Time was running out, and he needed a plan.

The cut across Julianne's face ached. But that pain was subdued by the threat of more pain. The blade of the knife sliced the outer layer of her skin, just enough for her to feel the prick.

"Nine," Alexandro called. Despite the cold, Julianne was suddenly sweating. Did she take matters into her own hands and try to elbow Alexandro?

Or did she let events play out as they would and pray for the best?

"Eight. Are you listening? It would be a shame to mess up her pretty face. Like you messed up her shoulder."

Her scar tightened, and a subtle throb began there. Darrell? Were they really talking about Darrell?

She had to get out of here, to get through this. There was so much she wanted to do. Mostly, she wanted to take life by the horns and stop living in fear. The first step of that would be to tell Bradley exactly how she felt about him. Even though Darrell wasn't in her life anymore, he'd still maintained a certain control over her. No more.

"Seven."

Her eyes scanned the woods, though she could see very little. Was Darrell out there? What would he do?

"Six."

Tension mounted in her shoulders. There was no way she could fight off this many men. One man, and maybe she might have a chance. A slim chance, but still. But four men? She just didn't see how it was possible, especially when at least one of them—probably more—had either knives or guns.

"Five." The knife cut deeper, hot pain searing into her. Tears popped to her eyes.

"I thought you cared about her, man. I thought

you were watching out for her, Darrell. I guess not. You're going to let her die for you." Alexandro paused. "Four."

Julianne listened for a movement, for a sign that something might change. Nothing.

And then something scattered and tumbled in the woods. A rock maybe? Definitely movement.

Alexandro relaxed his grip on her for a moment.

Suddenly someone stepped from the bushes, his hands raised in the air. Julianne blinked at the sight, wondering if the situation had just gotten better or worse.

Based on the terror that clutched her heart, this nightmare had just turned into something far worse than she could have ever imagined.

Bradley watched from behind the trees as Darrell stepped into the circle of men. There he was. Alive and untouched. He really had been behind all of this. But Bradley didn't have time to ponder that at this moment. Right now, he had to save Julianne.

Maybe Darrell would be just the distraction that Bradley needed to save Julianne.

He stayed put, trying to plan his next move carefully. There were a lot of men, and just one of him. If he took one shot at Alexandro, one of the other men could easily take a shot at Julianne.

"Don't kill her. I'm the one you want."

Julianne gasped, her eyes wide as her fiancé came into view.

He looked at her. "Hey there, sweetheart. Long time no see."

Alexandro stepped back from Julianne and sneered. "I knew this sénorita would be just the bait we needed. You owe us money. A lot of money. No one ever gets one over on the Amigos."

Darrell held his hands in the air. "You're right. I'm tired of running. But I don't have the money I owe you. I've been trying to get my hands on it for a long time now, but I haven't had any luck."

"Then I guess we'll just have to take your life instead."

Just as Alexandro raised his gun to Darrell's temple, Bradley took his first shot. The bullet hit Alexandro's hand, and he let out a curse. The other members of the Amigos turned, looking for the shooter. One by one, Bradley aimed and fired, hitting their shoulders—targeting places to injure them without death.

No, the authorities would want to talk to these men. Bradley wanted to talk to these men.

Darrell raised his hands as Bradley stepped from the trees. He kicked the guns away from each fallen Amigo's hand as he stepped into the circle, his weapon still hot in his hands. The police should be here any minute.

Though he wanted to reach for Julianne and

make sure she was okay, now was not the time. Right now, he had to focus on keeping her alive and safe. He motioned for her to stand beside him.

"Bradley Stone saves the day. Again." Darrell smirked. "You're good at doing that. You must really love Julianne to go through all of this trouble for her."

"I saw you die that day in training. How'd you fake your own death, Darrell? That's what I don't understand."

He shrugged, a new roughness about him. "I just found a homeless man who fit my description. I hid him out of sight the night before and put a uniform on him. I knew no one would suspect that it wasn't me. After the explosion, I hid in one of the buildings and waited until everyone cleared out. It was the longest twenty-one hours of my life. But finally I was able to sneak away and begin my new life." His gaze fell on Julianne. "But all I ever really wanted was to be with you."

Julianne shook her head. "And you didn't want anyone else to be with me, did you? That's why you kept killing any males who got close to me."

"I was trying to pave a way for us to be together again."

"We would have never been together again. Never."

"You were a fighter but I was determined to break you. You always fought back, though. I hated that I had to die before I finished the task." He curled his lips into a cocky smile. "The acid burn didn't seem to affect you as much as I'd hoped, so I figured I'd ruin your reputation, as well."

Bradley jerked his arm, pulling Darrell back from Julianne. "Why'd you kill Vanessa?"

The gleam left his eyes, replaced by that soulless expression again. "I broke into your home. I was going to steal some of those plans that I'd heard you talking about, the ones that your uncle had developed. I knew they'd be worth millions on the black market. I also knew that I could use that money to pay off some of my debt and to start a new life."

"But you didn't find the plans?"

"No, instead I found Vanessa. She recognized me. I didn't have any choice. It was a shame really. I always respected you, Commander."

"So you faked your own death to get the cartel off your trail. You owed them big money. Donald's life insurance policy hadn't been enough. Then you cashed out your own policy so you could live on your own. Meanwhile, you somehow managed to put Donald's body in your grave, knowing that the DNA match would be close."

He looked oddly impressed. "You guys caught up on all that rather quickly. The money from the life insurance policy ran out after a year."

"Then you killed your parents?" Julianne shook

her head, disgust evident in her gaze. "That's despicable, Darrell."

He shrugged. "A guy's gotta do what a guy's gotta do. They never liked me, anyway. Donald was the perfect son. They couldn't wait to get rid of me."

"Then you pulled Tommy Sanders into it? You knew about his indiscretions and blackmailed him to do the dirty work you couldn't do yourself." As Bradley said the words, the police surrounded them.

Darrell shrugged again, as if the situation didn't fluster him in the least. "Tommy did some drugs with me back when we were SEALs. He was involved with the cartel without even knowing it. I knew he'd be the perfect scapegoat. I wanted to make sure everything pointed to Tommy and not me."

Julianne shook her head again. "What would you do if you got Bradley's plans, Darrell?"

"Then I'd sell them to a terrorist organization—I still had plenty of contacts from when I was stationed over in the Middle East. I'd make big money from the deal. I'd be set for life—and beyond."

"And then what?" she asked.

"I'd pay off the Amigos, and then I'd be rich enough to buy an island and live out the rest of my life there. With you, preferably. If you weren't in jail by that time."

Bradley flexed his muscles as anger surged through him. How could one man be so evil? He'd never understand some people and the things they'd do for money. "You're one twisted man, Darrell."

Detective Spencer handcuffed him and led him away.

Bradley turned to Julianne. Her eyes were like saucers. She stepped closer, her hand going to his chest. "How'd you survive? The bullet...?"

He pulled his shirt back some. "Another new product we're developing—that bullet-proof vest I told you about earlier."

A sob caught in her throat, and she threw her arms around his neck, burying her face in his chest. "I'm so glad. I was so worried. I thought you were dead."

"I'm not. I'm sorry I accused you of those things. The nature of my job makes me perpetually suspicious. I should have trusted you more, but my emotions clouded my logic." He held her closer, deep sorrow making his heart heavy.

She stepped back and ran her fingers down the edge of his face. "I forgive you. I haven't exactly been one-hundred percent trusting of you, either. But I want to move past that. I want to move past all of this."

Bradley grinned. "Me, too."

"I was wondering if there might be a job opening at Eyes? I'm thinking about relocating."

"I think I know of an opening, but I've heard the boss can be a real bear sometimes."

She smiled up at him. "I think I'm up for the task."

He stroked her cheek, her hair, before finally his lips came down over hers. Peace and contentment spread through her, and, for the first time in years, excitement fluttered in her gut at the prospect of the future...of a future together with Bradley.

EPILOGUE

Julianne stood as the "Wedding March" began to play. She turned her attention to the door at the back of the church. A smile lit her face when she saw Elle begin down the aisle, looking gorgeous in a simple white wedding dress.

Bradley's hand went to her waist, and she smiled. She loved how he always made her feel as if she was treasured. The warmth of his hand crept through the material of her dress, making her glow from within.

As Elle reached the front of the church, Denton appeared on the stage, a huge grin across his face. That's what Julianne wanted. Someone whose eyes lit up when they saw her, who looked as if they'd won a million bucks whenever they were together.

Did she have that with Bradley? She thought so.

As they sat back down, Bradley's fingers intertwined with hers. She glanced up at him and smiled. It was hard to believe that only a few weeks ago they'd practically been strangers. Now it felt as if they'd known each other forever.

The ceremony was beautiful and touching, even if Julianne was having trouble paying attention.

It had been so long since she thought she had a shot at happiness. She didn't believe it could happen for her. But now, it seemed as if it could.

The rest of the wedding was splendid, and something about the ceremony caused a longing to stir in Julianne's heart. She wanted this one day.

She wanted this with Bradley.

The reception took place at a hotel on the beach. They stared out the floor-length windows that overlooked the Atlantic. Bradley wrapped his arms around Julianne as they waited for the new bride and groom to arrive.

"Julianne?" Bradley whispered in her ear.

"Yes?" Just the sound of his voice made her heart feel warm and full. She knew she'd found someone she could trust in Bradley. He allowed her to be herself, he never tried to control her, and always made her feel safe.

"Can I tell you something crazy?"

"Considering that I told you a crazy story a few weeks ago, and it ended up changing our lives, then sure. It's your turn now."

"I'm hoping this crazy thing I have to tell you might end up changing our lives also."

She turned around until she was facing him, and wrapped her arms around his neck. "What is it?"

"I love you, Julianne Grace. I know it's fast and that we haven't known each other that long. But I love you."

A smile stretched across her face. "You know what, Bradley Stone? I love you, too."

"I hope we can spend the rest of our lives trying to prove that to each other." He looked so sincere and honest and trustworthy. She wanted to look into those eyes for the rest of her life.

"I think I can make that happen."

He grinned and pulled her closer. His lips met hers, and happiness exploded inside Julianne. They'd weathered the storm together and grown stronger through the struggle.

Julianne knew she'd found a man who'd be her rock from now until eternity.

* * * * *

Dear Reader,

Like Julianne, there are times in life when everything seems to fall apart.

Friends may turn against you. Lies may be told about you. Those you trust may betray you.

Isn't it good to know that God is on our side? We can have confidence that God loves us. We can rest assured that God knows our heart—the good and the bad things—and accepts us, anyway.

Sometimes, in the midst of hardship, it's difficult to see that brighter days are ahead. Like Julianne, we must cling to the promises of God and trust that God truly is our stronghold forever.

Blessings,
Christy Barritt

Questions for Discussion

1. Julianne takes a chance at the beginning of the book and puts her life on the line in order to find answers. What kinds of things are you willing to take risks for?

2. Bradley is reminded that God calls us to care for the "least of these." What are some simple ways we can do this?

3. Julianne clings to Psalm 9:9, which says, "The Lord is a refuge for the oppressed, a stronghold in times of trouble." What does this verse mean to you?

4. Julianne is holding on to past hurts. Is there anything from the past that you're holding on to?

5. Bradley has buried himself in his work since his fiancée died. Are there ways that you pour yourself into certain activities in order to avoid reality or to avoid the hurts in your life? Is this healthy? What are some better ways to handle your pain?

6. Sometimes Julianne doubts herself. Do you ever doubt yourself? Why? How do you overcome those doubts?

7. In the midst of the storm, Julianne finds hope in God. What kind of storm are you in the middle of? How can you keep your gaze focused on Jesus?

8. Julianne found herself withdrawing as the result of a bad relationship. How do react when hard times hit? Do you withdraw or reach out?

9. Have you ever been blamed or accused of something you were innocent of? How did that feel? How did you handle it? What advice would you give someone else in those circumstances?

10. Have you ever felt like everyone's turned against you? Have you ever felt betrayed? Jesus felt the ultimate betrayal on the cross. How does this fact comfort you? How does the fact that Jesus died on the cross change your life?

REQUEST YOUR FREE BOOKS!

2 FREE WHOLESOME ROMANCE NOVELS IN LARGER PRINT

PLUS 2 FREE MYSTERY GIFTS

☀☀☀☀☀☀☀☀☀☀☀☀☀☀☀☀☀☀☀☀☀

HEARTWARMING™

✲✲✲✲✲✲✲✲✲✲✲✲✲✲✲✲✲✲✲✲✲✲

Wholesome, tender romances

YES! Please send me 2 FREE Harlequin® Heartwarming Larger-Print novels and my 2 FREE mystery gifts (gifts worth about $10). After receiving them, if I don't wish to receive any more books, I can return the shipping statement marked "cancel." If I don't cancel, I will receive 4 brand-new larger-print novels every month and be billed just $4.99 per book in the U.S. or $5.74 per book in Canada. That's a savings of at least 23% off the cover price. It's quite a bargain! Shipping and handling is just 50¢ per book in the U.S. and 75¢ per book in Canada.* I understand that accepting the 2 free books and gifts places me under no obligation to buy anything. I can always return a shipment and cancel at any time. Even if I never buy another book, the two free books and gifts are mine to keep forever.

161/361 IDN F47N

Name _____ (PLEASE PRINT)

Address _____ Apt. #

City _____ State/Prov. _____ Zip/Postal Code

Signature (if under 18, a parent or guardian must sign)

Mail to the **Harlequin® Reader Service:**
IN U.S.A.: P.O. Box 1867, Buffalo, NY 14240-1867
IN CANADA: P.O. Box 609, Fort Erie, Ontario L2A 5X3

* Terms and prices subject to change without notice. Prices do not include applicable taxes. Sales tax applicable in N.Y. Canadian residents will be charged applicable taxes. Offer not valid in Quebec. This offer is limited to one order per household. Not valid for current subscribers to Harlequin Heartwarming larger-print books. All orders subject to credit approval. Credit or debit balances in a customer's account(s) may be offset by any other outstanding balance owed by or to the customer. Please allow 4 to 6 weeks for delivery. Offer available while quantities last.

Your Privacy—The Harlequin® Reader Service is committed to protecting your privacy. Our Privacy Policy is available online at www.ReaderService.com or upon request from the Harlequin Reader Service.

We make a portion of our mailing list available to reputable third parties that offer products we believe may interest you. If you prefer that we not exchange your name with third parties, or if you wish to clarify or modify your communication preferences, please visit us at www.ReaderService.com/consumerchoice or write to us at Harlequin Reader Service Preference Service, P.O. Box 9062, Buffalo, NY 14269. Include your complete name and address.

HWDIR13R

ReaderService.com

Manage your account online!

- Review your order history
- Manage your payments
- Update your address

---

*We've designed
the Harlequin® Reader Service
website just for you.*

Enjoy all the features!

- Reader excerpts from any series
- Respond to mailings and
  special monthly offers
- Discover new series available to you
- Browse the Bonus Bucks catalog
- Share your feedback

Visit us at:
ReaderService.com